THE CURSE OF THE
INCREDIBLE PRICELESS CORNCOB

THE
COWDOG

THE CURSE OF THE
INCREDIBLE PRICELESS CORNCOB

John R. Erickson

Illustrations by Gerald L. Holmes

★
TexasMonthlyPress

Texas Monthly Press
P.O. Box 1569
Austin, Texas 78767

A   B   C   D   E   F   G   H

Library of Congress Cataloging-in-Publication Data

Erickson, John R., 1943–
  Hank the Cowdog and the curse of the incredible priceless corncob.
  ''The seventh exciting adventure in the Hank the Cowdog series.''
  Summary: While trying to outwit his arch enemy Pete the Barncat, Hank the Cowdog is duped into believing a worthless corncob will bring him fame and fortune.
  1. Dogs—Fiction. [1. Dogs—Fiction. 2. West (U.S.)—Fiction   3. Humorous stories] I. Holmes, Gerald L., ill.   II. Title.   III. Title: Curse of the in-credible priceless corncob.
PS3555.R428H29 1988 813'.54 [Fic] 88-29636
  ISBN 0-87719-142-5
  ISBN 0-87719-141-7 (pbk.)
  ISBN 0-87719-143-3

In Memory of My Aunt
Jonye Curry Patterson

Contents

CHAPTER
1

AN ASTRONOMY LESSON FOR THE DUNCE

It's me again, Hank the Cowdog. I'm still not sure how the corncobs fit into the overall case, or for that matter what part Pete the Barncat played in the mystery, but on the morning of September 7, at approximately ten o'clock, the cowboys roared into headquarters and called me up for Special Emergency Duty.

Little did I know what danger lay in store for me or that my very life would be hanging in the balance before the day was done. But then, that's getting the cart before the wagon.

Let's back up and take first things first. In the security business, you can get yourself in a mess trying to take first things second or second things first. First things should always be taken first.

1

Okay. Let's start with the corncobs.

On the evening of the morning before the day of which I speak. . . . Let's try that again. On the evening before the morning of the day of which . . . .

Might be simpler just to say, "On the evening of September 6." Okay, on the evening of September 6, Drover and I were down in the vicinity of the gas tanks, taking it easy and catching a few winks of sleep before we had to go out on night patrol.

As I recall the scene, I was reclined on my gunny sack bed, hovering in the twilight zone between watchfulness and more or less complete oblivion. In other words, although my more critical faculties were pretty muchly in neutral, I continued to monitor all sounds and earatory data in the Ready Room of my mind.

This is a trick of the trade, so to speak, that a guy builds up over a period of years. When you're on call twenty-four hours a day, when the safety of the ranch and all its inhabitants depends on your ability to scramble at the first sign of danger, you learn to grab your sleep when it comes and to remain alert even while sleeping.

Hencely, even though an outside observer

would have pronounced me asleep, the inner recesses of my mind continued to monitor incoming signals. A high percentage of those signals were coming from Drover, my associate, who sat nearby, staring up at the sky and composing dumb questions.

"Hank?"

My eyelids twitched but I tried to ignore him.

"Hank?"

"Um."

"You awake, Hank?"

I cracked my left eye and snapped a visual update for my data base, but this procedure met with only partial success since my left eye was still rolling around in its sprocket. Again, I tried to ignore him.

"Hank?"

"What!"

"You awake?"

"Of course it will! If it weren't for that, what else could it be?"

"What?"

"You heard what I said. Don't sit there pretending . . . what *did* I say?"

"I'm not sure."

"Well, if you're not sure, Drover, who is?"

"You got me."

"Then I've got very little. The question is, what is the meaning of this conversation?"

"I'm not sure, Hank. I just asked if you were awake."

"And what did I say?"

"That was the part I didn't understand."

That did it. I had no choice but to cancel the Sleep Mode and go back on duty. I opened both eyes and sat up.

"Drover, do you have any idea what you're talking about?"

"Not really. I was just trying to make conversation. I get bored sometimes."

"If I had to live with that tiny brain of yours, I'd get bored too."

"Yeah, but even though it's small, it's not very big."

"Don't try to argue with me. The point is that . . . what *was* the point?"

"I think we were trying to decide. . . . I'm not sure there was a point."

"Hence, by simple logic, we see that you've lured me into another pointless conversation. And you also woke me up, and don't try to deny it."

"Okay. Hank, you see the moon?"

I squinted my eyes and looked toward the

4

east and saw the alleged moon. "Of course I see the moon. Anyone with eyes can see the moon. I saw the moon at this same time last night and last month and last year. I assume, since that's such a stupid question, you'll follow it with another stupid question."

He shook his head. "No, that was all. I just wondered if you saw the moon."

I pushed myself up on all-fours and lumbered over to him. I was not in, shall we say, a jolly frame of mind. "Listen, pipsqueak, after interrupting my sleep, you'd better have another question in mind."

"Oh. Well, all right. Let me see here. Hank, how come the moon comes up in the evening and goes down after midnight?"

I stared at him and shook my head. "See? I knew you had one more stupid question in there. All right, I'll tell you, but I expect you to pay attention and remember your lessons. I don't want to go through this every night for the rest of our lives."

"Okay, Hank, I'm ready."

"Number one: hot air rises. Number two: cold air unrises, or you might prefer to say that it falls."

"Yeah, I like that better."

"Number three: the air at the end of the day

is hot. Number four: the air at the end of the night is cold. Can you figger it from there or do I have to fill in the blanks?"

He squinted one eye and thought about it. "Well, that tells me a lot about air but I was kind of curious about the moon."

"They're one and the same, you dunce."

"You mean the moon's nothing but air? I thought it was made out of cheese."

"It IS made out of cheese, but do you think it's up there hanging in water?"

"Well . . . no."

"Then what's it hanging in?"

Again, he squinted at the moon. "Right now, I'd say it's hanging in that big cotton-wood tree down by the creek."

"Absolutely wrong. It appears to be, but that's only a tropical illusion."

"It is? Then that means . . . "

"Exactly. It's actually hanging in thin air."

"It does look pretty thin."

"It's very thin, Drover, and since thin air is thinner than thick air and warm air is warmer than cool air, it follows from simple deduction that the moon rises. I can't make it any simpler than that."

"Oh, that's simple enough . . . I guess."

"Any more questions about the moon, the

sun, the planets, the canopy of stars that covers the skies at night? This is the time to ask your questions, Drover, while we're between investigations.''

"Well . . . what would happen if the moon was hanging in thin water instead of thin air? Would it sink or float?"

"That would depend on how thin the water was, and I think that's about all the time we have for questions. We've got work to do."

"I thought this was the time to ask questions."

"It was, but time marches on, and we either join the parade or go to the rodeo."

Drover scratched his ear. "I've never been to a rodeo."

"Yes, but you've never been to a parade either, so that only proves what I've said all along."

"What's that?"

"It's time to get to work. There's more to this life than rodeos and parades."

"I sure hope so. I've never been to either one."

I stared at the runt. "I just said that. Why are you repeating what I've already said?"

He hung his head. "I don't know. It just sounded good at the time, and I didn't know what else to say."

"Drover, when you don't have anything important to say, it's usually better just to keep your trap shut."

"Okay Hank, but it's liable to get awful quiet around here."

"That gives us something to hope for, doesn't it, and hope is the fuel for the machinery of life, so that pretty well wraps things up. Are you ready to go on patrol?"

"Well . . . I was feeling kind of sleepy, to tell you the truth."

"I appreciate the truth but the sleep will have to wait. We've got a job to do."

"Oh rats."

At that very moment, I heard the back door slam up at the house. I perked my ears and listened. Sally May's footsteps on the sidewalk, seventeen of them (seventeen footsteps, not seventeen sidewalks). Then, a fork scraping on a plate. Then . . .

"Kitty kitty kitty! Here Hank, here Drover!"

Ah ha! It was scrap time at the yard gate, one of my very favorite times of the day. "Come on, Drover. Our most important job right now is to beat the cat to the scraps. Let's move out."

We left the gas tanks and went sprinting up the hill.

Little did we know what awaited us at the top of the hill, and for the very best of reasons.

We weren't there yet.

[illegible] that are likely to go swimming [illegible] around there.

[illegible] something [illegible]

[illegible]

[illegible] the [illegible]

[illegible]

[illegible] I [illegible] and up at the [illegible] and [illegible] footprints on the sides all, seventeen of them [illegible] a plate [illegible]

[illegible] that it was some type of [illegible] is [illegible] out.

We left the [illegible] the hill.

[illegible] we know what [illegible] at the [illegible] of the hill and for the very [illegible] of reasons. We weren't there yet.

C H A P T E R

2

THE MYSTERY OF
THE CORNCOBS

Just as I had surmised, Sally May was standing at the yard gate with a plate in her hand.
And just as I had NOT surmised, Pete had beat
us there.

In other words, we had failed in our primary
mission of the evening, to beat the cat to the
scraps. Failure is painful enough by itself, but
when it comes at the hands of a cat, it becomes
almost unbearable, even though a cat has paws
instead of hands.

Drover and I couldn't have responded to the
call any faster, which left only one solution to
the puzzle: Pete had been tipped off about the
scraps. He had gotten inside information. In
other words, he had cheated, which is the typical cat method of doing business.

They don't play by the rules, see. They cheat and use sneaky behavior to compensate for certain design mistakes that were made when

G.L. Holmes

cats were first invented. When you deal with cats on a daily basis, as I do, you have to be prepared to play dirty.

Well, by the time we got there, Sally May had already scraped off one portion of scraps, and I don't need to tell you who was there to snatch them the instant they hit the ground: Mister Cheater, Mister Greediness, Pete the Barncat.

I went straight to him, figgered I'd check out his scraps to see exactly what he'd got. "Out of the way, cat. We're taking over this deal and you can run along and play."

Pete cut his eyes in my direction, pinned his ears down, and started growling and chewing at the same time. You ever notice how a cat does that? They come out with this peculiar sound, see, something between a yowl and a growl, but they're so greedy and stingy with food, they don't even bother to stop chewing.

That's what Pete did, and hey, there's just something about that kind of action that makes my temper jump about twenty degrees. Before I knew it, I was growling back at him.

And Drover, who was safely behind me and out of the range of Pete's claws, began jumping up and down. "Git 'im, Hankie, git 'im!"

I might very well have got him, I mean just

by George cleaned house right there while it was fresh on my mind, but Sally May reached across the fence and whacked me on the head with her spoon, sort of surprised me since I'd forgot she was there.

"You dogs get back and leave Pete alone! I'm going to feed you over here so you won't fight."

Pete rolled his eyes in my direction and gave me a grin. I backed off, but not until I had sniffed out his scraps: two steak bones and several nice long strips of steak fat, which happens to be a favorite of mine.

I love steak fat.

Sally May moved down the fence a ways and scraped our portion off the plate. When it hit the ground, I made a dive for it, scooped up a nice big bone, and began putting the old mandibles to work, so to speak.

That first taste of steak juice and steak fat sent waves of sheer joy rushing through my mouth, across my tongue, into my salvanilla glands, and on out to the end of my tail. I rolled the morsel around in my mouth for a moment and then sank my teeth into it and . . .

HUH?

Suddenly my mouth fell open and went blank, and the so-called steak scraps dropped out like a dead bird falling out of a tree. It hit the ground with a plop. I stared at it, sniffed it, checked it out.

I looked up at Sally May and wagged my tail. There had been some mistake. She had given me a baked potato hull. I gave her my most sincere, most hurtful look and wagged my tail extra hard.

I mean, I'm a very forgiving dog. I understand about mistakes. It would be no exaggeration to say that I've made several of them myself, in the course of a long and glorious career in security work.

Sure, I understood, and to help Sally May make a fair division of the scraps, I was willing to take a little extra time out of my busy schedule, walk down the fence, and redistribute some of the steak fat that Pete was growling and yowling over.

And I had every intention of sharing my baked potato hull with him too.

I started down the fence.

"HANK! You leave Pete alone. I won't have you beating up on the cat."

What ever gave her the idea that I was going

to. . . . "Now, you dogs have plenty to eat, and I'm going to stand right here until you eat it all up."

I went back to the spot. Okay, if a baked potato hull was the best I could get. . . . It was gone. My baked potato hull was gone! Someone or something had . . .

I looked at Drover. He swallowed something rather large and grinned.

"You just ate my baked potato hull, you idiot! I turn my back on you for just a minute and bingo! You're stealing my food. What next, Drover? Where do you go from being a common food thief?"

"Well . . . I thought you didn't want it."

"Of course I didn't want it, but it was still mine."

"I'm sorry, Hank, but I was hungry and . . . gosh, I feel so bad, I'll let you have all the rest of it."

"Well . . ." I thought it over. "At least you've got enough decency to make a gesture, and even though a gesture is only a gesture, it's no small potatoes either."

"No, I got the potatoes. You can have all the rest."

"That's exactly what I intend to do, Drover."

I moved into eating position above the scraps. Drover sat down a few feet away and watched me with a cock-eyed smile, while Sally May towered above me and watched with her arms crossed.

I took a large something into my mouth and began chewing. It was soft on the outside, hard on the inside, and tasted a bit like . . . well, corn. As a matter of fact, it tasted a lot like corn, and the more I chewed it, the cornier it tasted.

I rolled it around in my mouth and let it fall back to the ground. I stared at it. It was a corncob.

I lifted my head and searched Sally May's face for some answers. Had this been an accident? Was it some kind of joke? What did we have here? I wagged my tail and waited for an answer.

"Well," she said, "go on and eat it. If you can chew bones, you can chew corncobs. There's nothing wrong with them."

Let me break in here to point out that while Sally May was a wonderful lady in many respects, there were things she didn't understand about dogs. DOGS DON'T EAT CORNCOBS. I sniffed out the scraps one last time, drew my tail up between my legs, and, shall we say, vanished into the evening shadows. I hid in some tall weeds just above the gas tanks and watched to see what would happen next.

Sally May shook her head and said something about Hank being too fussy for his own good, and then she looked at Drover. "But *you'll* eat them, won't you, Drover? You're not a fussy eater, are you? Come here, puppy."

You know what the little dope did? He wagged and grinned his way over to the fence, collected his pat on the head, and then made a big show of eating a derned corncob. I could have wrung his neck.

He gummed the cob and rolled it around in his mouth and grinned up at Sally May, just as though he'd got hold of the best steak on the ranch—until Sally May went back into the house and turned off the yard light.

And then, why you'd have thought that cob was on fire, the way he spit it out! Once the audience goes home, the farce is over.

I came out of hiding and walked over to Drover. "That was a pretty good show you put on, son."

"Oh thanks, Hank. I didn't want Sally May to think we didn't like her corncobs."

"Yes, I noticed. It was a brilliant stroke. Now, for the rest of our lives, she's going to be feeding us corncobs and garbage, and thanks to you, she'll expect us to eat it!"

"Gee, I hadn't thought of it that way."

"That's too bad, son. You've made your bed and now the chickens will come home to roost in it."

"Oh my gosh, they're awful messy."

"Exactly. Well," I took a deep breath, "you've made a shambles of the evening. Let's see if we can salvage something of the night. Come on, we've still got two days' work to do between now and daylight."

We started down the hill. I had already begun sifting through details and organizing the night patrol, when all of a sudden I heard a sound that made me freeze in my tracks.

I froze in my tracks. Drover, who was looking at the stars, ran into me. "Hold up, halt! Did you hear what I heard?"

"Oops, 'scuse me, I don't know. What did you hear?"

"Shhh! Listen."

We cocked our heads and listened. There it was again, the sniveling, whining voice of a cat: "Ummm, they left all these nice corncobs, just for me!"

"So, it's all coming clear now," I whispered. "We've been duped by the cat. He engineered this whole thing just so he could steal our corncobs!''

"Huh. But I thought we didn't want the corncobs.''

"That's precisely what he wanted you to *think* you wanted, Drover. You played right into his devilish scheme, and I came within a hair of playing the sucker myself. But I think we've caught it just in the nick of time.''

"Oh good.''

"Come on, son, and prepare for combat. We're fixing to send Pete the Barncat to the School of Hard Knocks.''

And with that, we made an about-face and marched back up the hill.

CHAPTER

3

ANOTHER HUMILIATING DEFEAT FOR THE CAT

We stormed up the hill and caught Pete, just as he was about to help himself to our corncobs.

"That's far enough, cat, stop where you are, freeze, don't move a muscle, halt!"

Pete crouched down and began backing away from the cobs. "Uh oh, looks like the cops are here."

"You got that right, cat. I'd inform you of your constitutional rights if you had any, but you don't. All you have at this point in history is a bunch of trouble."

"Yeah," said Drover, "and you're in trouble too."

"Mmmm," said the cat, "I believe you're right."

21

"You almost pulled off your devious little scheme," I said, "but like all crinimals, you made a fatal mistake. Did you actually think you could work your medicine show and shell game on the Head of Ranch Security?"

"Well, I thought it was worth a try."

"Sometimes the crinimal mind amazes me. You had it all worked out, didn't you? You had everyone on the ranch playing his part and saying his lines. Oh, you're clever, Pete, but

G. L. Holmes

then you made your fatal mistake. Instead of waiting for a sucker to come along, you tried your scam on me!"

"Yeah," said Drover, "and on me too."

Pete shrugged and smiled. "We all have to work with what we've got."

"Exactly," I said, "and what you got was caught. Would you care to hear how I broke the case?"

"Might as well, if it's all the same price."

"Number one: I had a suspicion all along that something wasn't quite right. You were a little too eager and a little too greedy in eating your steak scraps. In other words, you over-played your part."

"Oh shuckins."

"And number two: as we were walking away, we overheard your smart aleck remark. In other words, you just couldn't resist mouthing off. That was your fatal flaw, Pete. You blew the case wide open with your own big mouth."

"Yeah," Drover chimed in, "and now we want our corncobs back."

Pete grinned. "Oh no, I'm afraid we can't do that. You boys walked away from them and now they're mine. Finders keepers, losers weepers."

I gave him a growl. "You're going to be the losers' sweeper, cat, 'cause I'm fixing to sweep the ranch with your carcass. Get away from our cobs."

His eyelids hung low over his eyes and he started twitching the end of his tail. "Now hold on, Hankie, I'm sure we can work something out. I'll trade you the last piece of steak fat for your interest in the cobs."

I was about to reject the deal out of hand, but then I caught myself. Hmmm. I sure did like steak fat. "There's very little chance we can work out a trade, cat, but let's see what you've got."

I followed him over to the spot near the gate where he had made a pig of himself. Sure enough, there was a four-inch strip of steak fat lying on the ground, and it appeared to be cooked just the way I like it. Furthermore, a short distance away was a T-bone that still had plenty of meat on it.

I must admit that the fumes coming off the steak fat had a powerful effect on my smello-metric apparatus, so much so that I was almost by George overwhelmed by it. I had to take a step backward and turn my nose away from the fumes, else I would have lost my head.

"Well," said the cat, "what do you think,

Hankie? Isn't that a pretty piece of steak fat?"

"I've seen better," I lied. "Stay here, cat, don't move. I want to have a conference with my assistant."

Pete shrugged and began licking his paw. Drover and I went off to ourselves and held a short meeting.

"What do you think, Drover?"

"Oh, I want to trade! If he's dumb enough to give us steak fat for a couple of corncobs, I think we ought to go for it."

"Yes, I know what you mean, but there's something about this whole thing that still bothers me. Look at him, Drover." We watched Pete licking down some rough hair on the back of his right rear leg. He appeared very cool and confident. "That cat's too sure of himself. He thinks he's got the upper hand."

"Well, he's wrong about that, Hank. Anybody can see that he's got the lower leg."

"Exactly my point, Drover. I think he's running a bluff. I think he's still got some flex in his deal, and it's our job to smoke him out."

"Well, maybe so, but I sure like steak fat better than corncobs."

"Of course you do, but you can't let the cat know it. You don't understand trading, Drover. It's a science all to itself. It takes tremendous discipline and self-control. Watch me and study your lessons.''

I swaggered over to Pete. ''We've discussed your deal, and there's no way we can let those corncobs go for one measly strip of steak fat. It's a bad trade and you know it.''

Pete stood up and yawned and started rubbing against the fence. ''Well, it was worth a try.''

''Yes, it was worth a try, Pete, and if you had proposed that deal to a couple of ordinary mutts, you probably could have pulled it off. But you're not dealing with ordinary mutts.''

''Yes, I can see that.''

''So, to bring you up to date, we're rejecting your offer and breaking off the negotiations. Unless . . . ''

His eyes widened and his ears twitched—just the sort of clues a sharp negotiator looks for. I had pitched out some bait, and he had made the mistake of going for it.

''Yes, go on. Unless what, Hankie?''

''Unless,'' I walked around, looked up at the sky, took my good sweet time, see, which always impresses them, ''unless you threw that steak bone into the deal, and that just might send us back to the bargaining table. I'm not making any promises, but the bone would definitely sweeten the pot."

Pete studied me for a long time, and all at once I could see respect and admiration in those cat eyes which usually expressed only cunning, sneakiness, arrogance, and the kind of smug self-satisfaction that makes cats so hard to bear.

This cat had met his match in all categories. It was written all over his face.

"Mmmm, you drive a hard bargain, Hankie."

I chuckled. "When you're holding aces, Pete, you bet the limit. You know that. I know that. Everyone in this crazy business knows that. Now, what'll it be: stay or fold?"

"I'll take it."

I could hardly believe my ears. He had just agreed to trade me *a piece of steak fat and a T-bone for two corncobs?*

I studied his face again, especially the eyes. The eyes tell it all, don't you know. His had that shifty look again, and my cowdog instincts told me to go slow. "Not so fast, cat. We'll need to take this up in executive session."

Drover and I went off to the side again.

Drover was jumping up and down as if he had little springs on all four feet. "Boy, you sure put it to him, Hank, I didn't think he'd ever go for it but you sure put one over on him this time!"

"Be quiet a minute, let me think."

Drover quit hopping around and stared at me. "What's there to think about?"

We observed a moment of silence. "Can you see what he's doing, Drover?"

"Yeah, he's getting skinned!"

"I thought so too—at first. But there's a pattern to all this, and at last I've figured out what he's up to. Why would he trade good steak scraps for two worthless corncobs?"

"I don't know and I don't care. Let's eat, I'm starved."

"Not so fast. You're walking right into his trap. The truth is that those corncobs are *priceless* and Pete will stop at nothing to get his hands on them. I would guess that they're worth their weight in diamonds and rubies."

"But who wants to eat diamonds and rubies!"

"Exactly. We'd be fools to try, and we'd be bigger fools to trade Priceless Corncobs for a miserable pile of steak scraps. Drover, if you agree, I'm going to pull out of the negotiations."

"Oh good, 'cause I don't agree."

"You're sure about that?"

"Absolutely sure."

"In that case, I have no choice but to pull rank and disqualify your vote. If you insist on stinking with your thomach . . . thinking with your stomach, that is, then you must expect to lose some of your privileges. But remember, Drover: I'm doing this for your own good."

"Oh. Well, that's a different matter. I thought maybe you'd just made a dumb mistake."

"Almost, Drover. I almost traded away our fortune, which would have ranked as the dumbest mistake of the year, but our fortune is safe. We have managed to snatch defeat out of the jaws of tragedy, so to speak."

"Well, that's a relief."

"Indeed it is. Now, all we have to do is break the bad news to Pete. I'll do the talking. If he puts up a struggle, we'll go into a Code Three. You got that?"

"I think so. Let's see, a Code Three's between Code Two and Code Four."

"We don't have a Code Four."

"Oh yeah."

"Just stay behind me if something breaks loose, and don't get hurt. Let's move out."

We crept back to the fence, but instead of going directly to Pete, I took up a defensive position between him and the Priceless Corncobs. I didn't think he was foolish enough to start something, but with cats you never know.

"All right, cat, listen carefully and do exactly as I say and no one will get hurt. The deal's off. We're taking the treasure down to the gas tanks. Keep your paws where I can see them and don't make any sudden moves. Drover, get one of the Priceless Corncobs and go on down to the tanks. I'll keep the cat covered."

"Okay Hank." He picked up half the treasure and vanished in the darkness.

Smiling at the cat, I backed away. "You almost pulled it off, Pete. I've got to hand it to you. When it comes to being sneaky and devious, you're the champ. You were one step ahead of me right up to the end, but then you were undone by your own greed."

He looked at his claws. "I might sweeten the deal a little more."

"No way, Pete. As you know very well,

these corncobs are worth a fortune. Now, just stay where you are while I . . . "

I snatched up the remaining Priceless Corncob and made a dash down the hill to the gas tanks.

And suddenly, for the first time in my career, I was a wealthy dog.

CHAPTER

4

THE SEED OF GREED TAKES ROOT IN DROVER'S TINY BRAIN

I joined Drover down at the gas tanks, and we spent the next half hour in a wild celebration.

"Drover, do you have any idea what we've just pulled off?"

"Sure do."

"What have we just pulled off?"

"Well . . . I know we've pulled off something, but maybe you could refresh my memory."

"What we've pulled off, Drover, is the deal of the year, the deal of the century. Do you realize how wealthy you are at this moment?"

"Not really."

I lay back on my gunny sack and looked up

33

at the stars. "Drover, half an hour ago you were just another flunky ranch dog, but now you're worth your weight in gold, silver, diamonds, pearls, rubies, steak bones, or any other commodity you'd care to use as a standard of wealth."

"How about sleep? That's about the best thing I know."

"Good point. Yes, Drover, you're now worth your weight in sleep. Tell me, pardner, how does it feel to be filthy rich?"

"Gosh, I'm not sure. I've been filthy before but never rich. How's it supposed to feel?"

"Well, you understand that I haven't had much practice at this either, but I think a guy's supposed to notice a difference. I guess one thing you do when you're rich is you spend a lot of time thinking about your money."

"Yeah, but we don't have money. We have corncobs."

"*Priceless* Corncobs, Drover, and that's better than money. I mean, what could we do with money?"

"I don't know." There was a moment of silence. "What can we do with corncobs?"

"*Priceless* Corncobs and . . . " I thought for a long time. "By George, we can look at them, Drover."

G.L. Holmes

"We sure can. Let's do it."

I nosed my Incredible Priceless Corncob into position, a couple of feet west of my gunny sack. Then I sat down and looked at it.

35

Drover followed my lead and did the same. For a long time we didn't say a word, just sat there looking at our Incredible Priceless Corncobs.

I broke the silence. "Beautiful, aren't they?"

"Sure are."

"You ever see anything so beautiful in your whole life?"

"Well . . . it still looks a little like a corncob to me, Hank."

"You're not concentrating. Think of it as wealth, Drover. Think of it as the answer to your every dream and wish."

"Okay, I'm going to concentrate." He concentrated.

"Now what do you see?"

"Oh my gosh, it's beautiful, Hank!"

"See? What did I tell you? It's fame, it's fortune, it's freedom, it's power and influence and handsome good looks."

"Yeah, I see it all now."

"It's other dogs addressing you as Sir. It's respect from the cowboys. It's the women falling all over you."

"Even Beulah?"

I studied the runt out of the corner of my eye. "Beulah will be too busy falling all over me. She won't have time for you."

"Oh rats."

"But there are other women, Drover, hundreds of them, thousands of them, and they'll be fighting each other to get a lock of your hair for their scrapbooks."

"No fooling? That might hurt."

"Beauty knows no pain, Drover. Take my word for it. When those ladies start turning handsprings over you, you won't worry about losing a little hair."

"Maybe not. Boy, I can hardly wait. Do they come here or do we have to go to them?"

"Oh, it varies. We'll just have to see how things shape up. But it wouldn't surprise me at all, Drover, if a couple dozen lady dogs show up here, once the word gets out."

"Oh my gosh. And all because of a corncob?"

"An Incredible Priceless Corncob, and the answer to your question is yes."

"Gee, we're liable to have a hard time running the ranch when all the women show up. In fact . . . aren't we supposed to be on night patrol right now?"

I filled my lungs with fresh night air and ran my eyes over the beautiful Incredible Priceless

Corncob in front of me. "That's the way we used to operate, Drover, before we came into this wealth. But you know what?"

"What?"

"I don't want to go on night patrol. I want to sit right here on my gunny sack and look at my fortune. And you know what else?"

"What else?"

"That's exactly what I'm going to do. Why should I go out and risk my life for this outfit? What's in it for me?"

"Co-op dog food, I guess."

"Exactly. Co-op dog food. Who needs it? I've got a fortune sitting right here in front of me."

"Yeah, but you can't eat it."

"Who needs to eat? *We're rich, Drover!* All we have to do is sit right here and gloat over our fortunes. Isn't that what you've always wanted to do?"

"Well . . . that depends on what gloat means."

"Gloat means," I rolled over on my back and snuggled down into my gunny sack and kicked my paws in the air, "gloat means to be unbearable and obnoxious. That's what you're supposed to be when you're rich."

"Aw heck, really?"

"That's right. So what we're going to do tonight is loll around, goof off, admire our fortunes, and gloat."

"And let the ranch go to pot?"

"Well, maybe not go all the way to pot, but it wouldn't surprise me if it took a couple of steps in that direction. And so what, Drover? Just so what?"

Drover rolled his eyes around. "That sure doesn't sound like you, Hank. I never heard you say things like that before."

"I've never been rich before, and I've never had a fortune to sit around and admire. Speaking of which . . . " I rolled over on my belly and lay there, gazing at my glittering fortune.

Drover did the same, only after a couple of hours, he fell asleep. I could hear him wheezing and see him twitching in his sleep.

"Hey! Wake up."

"Huh, I'm coming, don't, my leg hurts . . . " He stared at me for a good thirty seconds. It took that long for his eyes and ears to straighten out. "Oh, it's you."

"That's correct, and speaking of whom, I gave you time off to admire your fortune, so how come you fell asleep?"

"Oh . . . I guess I got bored, Hank. Don't you think it's a little boring, just sitting here, staring at a corncob?"

I sighed and shook my head. "We've been over this before, Drover. What you have in front of you is not a mere corncob. It's a rare and priceless object. But then, you always did have a little trouble with the cultural side and . . ."

An idea began to form in my head. My gaze prowled the area in front of his bed and fastened upon his cob. "Tell you what I might do, Drover. If that old corncob is getting in your way over there, I could always, shall we say, take it off your hands."

That got his attention. He snatched up his Priceless Corncob and moved several feet to the north. And he kept himself between me and his fortune.

"No thanks. I can take care of it myself."

I watched him for a long time. Every now and then, he turned his head around to see what I was doing. All at once he was behaving in a very suspicious manner. There was just something about the way he looked at me . . .

Then it hit me: Drover didn't trust me. It's common knowledge that crooks show themselves in their lack of trust for others. In other words, the fact that Drover didn't trust me was a clear warning that I shouldn't trust him either.

And come to think of it, I didn't.

I moved my Priceless Corncob several feet to the south and placed myself between it and Drover. Every now and then I would glance back over my shoulder and catch Drover snealing steaky glances at me, stealing sneaky glances at me.

It was pretty obvious that he had something on his mind.

It must have been past midnight when I heard him trying to sneak off into the night. I called to him and asked him where he was going.

"Oh, just going for a little walk."

When his footsteps faded into the distance and I was sure he had gone, I eased myself up and slipped over to the spot where he had been guarding his Priceless Corncob—just as a precaution, don't you see, to make sure that, uh, nobody came along and stole it.

Well, here's a shocker. It was already gone! *He had snuck off into the darkness to hide it!* And from whom do you suppose he was hiding it from who? Whom. Whatever.

Well, that told me a lot about my assistant

that I hadn't known before, hadn't wanted to know. It told me that fortune was going to Little Drover's head. He was getting ate up with GREED.

You hear about that sort of thing all the time but you always think it happens to the other guy. But let me tell you, when you see it in somebody close to you, a good friend and business associate, it hurts.

Well, after the initial pain and shock of this discovery had soaked in, it dawned on me that I would have to take steps to protect my own fortune from . . . well, we needn't name names. I had to protect it from vandals and thieves, so to speak, and I wouldn't be able to sleep a wink until I had it safely buried.

Drover came back just as I was slipping away. "Hank? Where you going?"

"Oh, just thought I'd take a walk and soak up some night air."

I didn't wait to hear his answer. I shot through the night, flying over the ground on feet that made only the merest whisper of a sound.

My fortune was in danger, fellers, and I had to take steps to protect it.

CHAPTER

5

THE PLOT GETS THICKER, SO TO SPEAK

It's too bad when you can't trust your own assistant. But that just shows that some dogs can handle wealth and some can't.

It became pretty clear to me that the Incredible Priceless Corncob was going to make Drover jealous, petty, suspicious, and greedy, and I couldn't ignore the possibility that during the night he would try to steal my fortune.

I wanted nothing to do with that, so I slipped away from the gas tanks and went out to find a safe place to hide it.

I'd already thought this deal over, see, and figgered the best place to bury my treasure was in Sally May's garden. Nobody would ever think to look there for buried treasure and . . . well, you might say that the ground was

43

softer in the garden. Easier digging, don't you see.

A dog in my position has better things to do than to claw holes in hard ground. Part of good ranch management lies in, I think you get the point.

So I headed straight for the garden. At the hogwire fence, I stopped, listened, looked over both shoulders, hopped the fence, and landed in the okra, kind of hurt, actually. At that time of year, okra plants are pretty tough.

I slipped through the okra, past the black-eyed peas, over the cucumbers, around the squash, between two tomato plants, and I started digging.

I've always been a pretty good digger, when I put my mind to it, and it didn't take me long to build a hole. I dropped the Priceless Corncob into it and had just started nosing dirt back in, when I heard a snig twap. Twig snap.

I froze, cocked my head, and raised my right ear (I'm right-eared, don't you know, it's my best one). I listened and heard the merest whisper of a sound out there in the darkness. Yes, there it was again.

That's when I realized that I had been followed by bandits. I had no way of knowing how many there were, but my best guess placed the number between three and five, with a chance of the number going as high as six.

Six-to-one is what I consider farmable, formable . . . formidable odds. In other words, when the enemy holds that kind of advantage, only an idiot would try to fight his way out. It's a real good time to use cunning instead of brute strength.

I knew they were after my Priceless Corncob, and I knew they would stop at nothing to get it. I had met their kind many times before, and I hoped I could work out a strategy that would not only save my fortune but also my life.

I went on with my work, just as though I had heard nothing. I nosed the dirt into the hole and made a big show of leaving the spot. Going back through the garden, I made plenty of noise. Then I jumped the fence and pretended to be heading back to the gas tanks.

But, as you may have already suspected, I didn't. I made a wide circle and came in behind the robbers. But now, instead of snapping twigs and making noise, I was moving in Silent Mode.

The moon had climbed up in the sky and it was throwing out enough light so that I could see the profile of one of the bandits.

He was just sitting there near the base of one of those big Chinese elms, looking off toward the garden. He appeared to be a small-to-medium-sized dog with short white hair.

So far, so good. But where were his companions? I gave the area a thorough visual sweep which turned up nothing but the one dog.

Yes, it was all fitting together. Within seconds, I had analyzed the data and broken the code, so to speak, of their plan of attack. They had split up and left this one dog as a look- out. The other five or six bandits were somewhere between the garden and the calf shed.

My job was to pick them off one by one, starting with the lookout. If I did the job right, I could neutralize their advantage of superior numbers.

I got down in my crouch and moved forward. With each step, I paused to check the enemy and see if he suspected anything. Nothing. Either he was deaf or my Silent Mode was working to perfection.

I closed the gap between us until I reached Attack Range 1, at which time I coiled my legs,

46

sprang up and outward, and flew through the air like an enormous arrow.

I struck the enemy with all four paws, just buried him under an avalanche of pure muscle

G.L. Holmes

and slashing teeth. He never saw it coming, never knew what hit him, he was just by George . . .

"Hank, help, mayday, attack, murder, oh my gosh!"

There was something strangely familiar about that voice. I was sure I had heard it before, and not so very long ago. I called up a memory search of all the gangsters I had gone up against in the past year, trying to match the voice with a face.

Within seconds, I came up with a match—not exactly the one I had expected. Imagine my surprise when the robber turned out to be none other than my professional associate. That's correct. I had caught Drover in the act of trying to steal my treasure.

I had him on the ground between my front paws when I made a positive identification. All at once I felt sick, weak. Maybe I should have gone ahead and whipped him, but this terrible revelation had taken the fight out of my sails.

I looked down at him. When his eyes finally popped open, our gazes met. "Oh Hank, it's you!"

"No, Drover, you got it backward. It's YOU."

"Well, I knew it was me but now I can see it's you too, so I guess it's one or the other."

I stepped off of him and moved a few steps away. "Get up and prepare to answer some hard questions."

He hopped up and gave me that simpleton smile of his. "Okay, I'm ready, ask me anything, boy, I thought I'd been attacked by a mountain lion, sure am glad it was you."

"By the time I finish this interrogation, you'll wish it had been a mountain lion. Question number one: What are you doing out here, creeping around in the dark?"

"Who me? I wasn't exactly creeping, Hank . . ."

"Answer the question."

"Oh. Well . . . " He looked up at the moon. "Do I have to tell the truth or can I fudge a little bit?"

"The truth, the whole truth, and nothing but the truth."

"All three at once?"

"That's correct."

"Oh shucks. Well, Hank, when you left the gas tanks, I sort of got suspicious that you might be going out to dig up my corncob, so I decided to follow you . . ."

"Hold up, stop right there. Are you telling me that you buried your Incredible Priceless Corncob?"

"Yeah, in the garden."

"Why did you choose the garden?"

"Well . . . it's easier to dig there, I guess."

"In other words, you were too lazy to dig a proper hole, is that what you're saying?"

"I guess that's one way to put it."

"All right, next question." I began pacing. "Why did you feel you had to bury your treasure? I mean, there has to be a reason for these things."

"Well . . . I was afraid somebody might steal it."

"Now we're getting to the meat of the heart. Who or whom did you think might steal this alleged treasure of yours?"

"Oh . . . well . . . you never can tell . . ."

Suddenly I stopped pacing and whirled on him. "Shall I say it for you, Drover? Is it too painful for you to confront your own wicked thoughts? You thought I might steal your fortune, didn't you?"

"Well . . . sort of."

"Me! The Head of Ranch Security, your trusted friend and companion. And so you took your treasure out into the night and buried it in the garden because you were too lazy and shiftless to dig a hole in a better place. Is that it, Drover?"

His head began to sink. "Well . . . "

"Furthermore, we can't ignore the possibility that your real motive in coming out here was to spy on me while I buried MY treasure in the garden."

"You buried yours too?"

"In which case you're not only guilty of being suspicious of me, but also of plotting to steal my treasure."

"I didn't even think of that."

"Of course you did. Down deep, in your most secret heart, you were plotting to steal my fortune and leave me penniless."

"I was?"

"Yes. Do you see what wealth has done to you, Drover? It's driven a sledge between us. It's turned friend against friend, brother against brother."

"I guess you're right. That's pretty bad, isn't it?"

"Yes, Drover, that's pretty bad. However," I stopped pacing and studied the claws on my right paw, "there is a solution."

"There is?"

"Yes. If you insist, I will save you from

temptation, suspicion, greed, and temptation."

"You said temptation twice."

"Because it's twice as dangerous."

"Oh. Well, it sounds pretty good to me."

"How can you say that temptation sounds good to you!"

"No, I mean your deal."

"Oh yes, the deal. Yes, it's an excellent deal. All you have to do is turn over your corncob to me."

He gave me a blank stare. "You mean give it up?"

"What you will be giving up, Drover, is the source of many of your problems."

"Oh. But won't I be penniless then?"

"In a sense, yes. But what would you do with a penny if you had one?"

"I don't know. I just didn't want to be penniless."

"Yes, I see what you mean. Tell you what we can do, Drover. You give me the corncob and I'll owe you a penny. As long as someone owes you a penny, you can't possibly be penniless."

He scratched his ear and thought it over. "That sounds reasonable."

"Of course it's reasonable, why don't we

mosey over to the garden, it's going to spare you a lot of grief and if you'll just show me where you buried that old cob, we'll have everything fixed up." I started toward the garden but he didn't move. "What's the matter?"

"Well, it sounds reasonable, Hank, but I think I'll hang on to that old corncob."

I glared at him. "In spite of what it's doing to your personality? You would actually risk our friendship over one measly corncob?"

"Oh heck no. But I think I'd do it for my Priceless Corncob."

"I see, yes. Very well, Drover. I can't tell you how disappointed I am."

"Oh good."

"You've made this decision. Now you'll have to sleep in it."

"Yeah, I'm kind of tired."

"So if you'll remain exactly where you are, I shall return to the garden and retrieve my fortune. When I've gone, you may go get yours."

"Okay, and then I'll go get mine."

"Exactly." I started backing toward the garden. "I had hoped it wouldn't end this way, Drover, and don't ever say that I didn't try to save you from yourself."

"I won't tell anybody if you won't."

"So long, Drover. I hope you can live with yourself after this."

"Me too. I wouldn't know where to go if I couldn't."

Suddenly, I turned and sprinted into the darkness, leaped over the garden fence, and saved my Priceless Corncob from the greedy clutches of a former friend.

CHAPTER
6

CHOSEN FOR A
VERY DANGEROUS
ASSIGNMENT

I left the garden and went down to the creek.
There I dug a large hole in the soft sand and
buried my sparkling, glittering, enormous, incredible fortune.

At last it was safe. At last I would be able to
sleep. I started back to the gas tanks.

But then the thought occurred to me: what
if the creek came up in the night and washed
my treasure away? No, that wasn't a good hiding place. I went back and dug up my treasure.

This time I chose a spot in the feed barn,
over against the north wall behind a bale of
prairie hay. Nobody would ever look in the
feed barn for a treasure. I started back to the
gas tanks, confident that . . .

What if the coons raided the feed barn? WHAT IF THEY WERE ALREADY THERE!

I didn't have a minute to lose. I turned and dashed back to the feed barn, wiggled through the place at the bottom where the door is warped (almost cut off the lower half of my body in the process), and, to my great relief, found that I had gotten there just in time.

The treasure was safe.

I moved it down to the sick pen and slipped it under one of those old wooden feed troughs. Surely it would be . . . but maybe not. Hadn't I left tracks in the dirt? Anyone who leaves tracks in the dirt can be tracked.

No, my treasure wasn't safe there. I removed it and went in search of a better hiding place.

I must have walked around headquarters five times before it dawned on me that a safe hiding place simply did not exist. I mean, if you're hiding garbage or ordinary stuff, any old place will do, but if you're hiding a priceless fortune . . .

Of course that left me with a small problem. What the heck was I going to do with it if I couldn't hide it? I didn't dare leave it anywhere, I didn't dare sleep, I didn't dare let it out of my grasp, so you might say that I

walked around all night with the Priceless
Corncob in my mouth.

Sure got sleepy. Boy, did I get sleepy. Could
hardly keep my ice open, but iron discipline
pre vailed and I kepp ppinch ing mys   self to
sssstay   awakzzz   derned   near
fell   slee   p   zzzzeveral   time
zzzzzzzzzzzzzzzzzzzzzzzzzzzz

H U H??

All at once, someone was bending down,
yelling in my face! Who was this man? What
was the meaning of this? He must have been in-
sane, yelling at me like that.

Well, hey, if there's anything I can't stand,
it's one thing more than another, and also crazy people yelling at me in the morning, so I by
George bristled up and . . .

Morning?

How could it be morning? IT COULDN'T BE
MORNING! I remembered very distinkingly
. . . only moments ago . . . through iron discipline I had . . . I'll be a son of a gun, it WAS
morning.

And the guy yelling in my face was High
Loper. "Hank, wake up, you lazy devil, we've
got a job for you! Come on, jump in the
pickup!"

Job for me . . . jump in the pickup, by

57

George okay, I was wibe awape and reaby to go worp, I jumped up and staggered five steps and leaped into the back of the pickup, my leaper didn't work so good, hit the tailgate dead center with my nose, derned near broke it off, hit the ground hard, jumped up, tried her again, got her done this time, landed slap in the middle of the pickup bed and also on the high-lift jack.

G. L. Holmes

And by that time I was not only wide awake but I realized that I had fallen asleep sometime during the night, which is sort of a precondition to waking up. Falling asleep, that is.

I could hardly believe it. How could I have . . . well, I never claimed to be more than flesh and blood.

I yawned and took a big stretch. And then I remembered MY TREASURE. My eyes darted to the spot where I had fallen asleep.

THE PRICELESS CORNCOB WAS GONE! Someone or something had stolen it in the night, and although I hated to cast dispersions at anyone in particular, my cowdog intuition told me that Drover had . . .

Oh. It was then I noticed that Slim had come along, picked up the cob, and was taking it to the trash barrel. He pitched it into one of the three barrels and wandered over to the pickup.

Well, that wasn't exactly a catastrophe. All I had to do was hop out of the pickup, slip over to the barrel . . .

"Hank, get back in the pickup!"

On the other hand, maybe I could wait until we got back from this job. I hopped back in the pickup bed and greeted Loper with a friendly wag and big cowdog smile.

He started the pickup and we went roaring

up the hill in front of the house. Drover, also known as Mister Sleep Till Noon, heard the noise and managed to lift his head off his gunny sack for just a second. He looked around, waved goodbye, and went back to sleep.

No big surprise there. That's typical Drover. But you'll notice that the cowboys chose ME for this important job, not Mister Half-Stepper.

They can tell who hustles and who's a slacker. Also who's a greedy-gut and who's not.

Anyway, we went up the hill and past the front of the house. Little Alfred was out in the front yard and waved a yellow sand shovel at us.

That's one of the little bonuses of being on the first string, don't you see. When you're chosen for an important mission, you can ride on the spare tire in the back of the pickup and watch the little kids wave and cheer as you go off to the pasture.

Kids kind of idolize a brave and heroic cowdog, which is one of the bonuses I guess I already said that.

We pulled around to the back of the machine shed and Loper backed up to the green stock trailer. Slim got out and signaled him back, flopping his hands for "left," then

"right," then "come on back," then . . .
crunch!

Slim shook his head. "That's a little too much."

Loper watched him in the rear-view mirror. "How am I supposed to know what all your dadgum hand signals mean!"

"Pull up!"

"You just told me to come back!"

"Well, come back then, I don't care. But if you want to hook up this trailer, you'll have to *pull up*."

Loper grumbled and stuck the gear shift into grandma-low and crept forward. To help him out, I barked a couple of times. "Hank, shut up!"

O-kay.

"Whoa!" Slim called out, then he shook his head and frowned. "No, that's too much now. Back up."

"Make up your mind, will you! We've got work to do."

Loper put the pickup into reverse and came back. Slim measured off the distance between his hands and clapped them together.

"There you go. Hold her right there." On impulse, I barked again. Slim's eyes came up.

He grinned and shifted his chewing tobacco over to the other cheek. "Loper wouldn't go very far in this life without our directions, would he, Hank?" I barked three more times.

Loper stuck his head out the window and launched some tobacco juice into the weeds. "Are you welding that trailer or just hooking it up? Come on, we're burning daylight!" I barked for that. "Shut up, Hank."

Slim cranked the trailer down on the hitch ball and locked it in place. He didn't hook up the trailer lights, I noticed. These guys never hook up the trailer lights because the trailer lights never work.

Poor management, if you ask me.

Slim climbed into the cab and off we went. I climbed on top of the spare tire so's I could catch a nice fresh breeze on my face and see where we were going.

That's one of my jobs around here, riding look-out. Any cars or trucks that come along need to be barked. You never know who might be riding in those cars and trucks, and the best policy is to give them a good barking right away.

Loper turned right at the mail box and then made a left onto that pasture road that goes up into the canyons. I sat up there on the spare tire and enjoyed one of God's blessings, a nice fresh fall breeze blowing over my . . .

By George, it was raining. I got a big juicy raindrop right in the middle of my face, is how I knew it was raining. But there was something funny about this rain.

I studied the sky. There wasn't a cloud up there, not even one. I had just about decided that I had imagined the raindrop when another one smacked me just below the left ear, and before I knew it, another one smacked me just below the right ear.

You know what? Them raindrops were brown. Never saw anything quite like it. I checked the clouds again and caught two more raindrops square in the face.

That was enough for me. I went to the back of the pickup. I can't tell you what makes brown raindrops fall out of a clear blue sky, but I can tell you from firsthand experience that if you go back to the tailgate and lie down, the rain will stop.

Beats anything I ever saw.

CHAPTER

7

A NARROW ESCAPE WITH HORNED DEATH

We made our way north over that dusty, bumpy road, climbed the caprock, went into the middle pasture, followed the road where it loops around to the west, turned back north over at the fence between the middle and west pastures, drove a mile or two in that direction, and went into the northwest pasture at that wire gate near the spot where that old cow died in the blizzard and her bones are still there, which explains why they call it Dead Cow Gate.

Sounds kind of spooky, doesn't it? Dead Cow Gate. Well, if you think that's spooky, I've got some bad news for you. The REAL spooky part is yet to come.

I mean, unbeknownst to me, I had been

tapped for one of the most dangerous missions of my career, and if you have the slightest physical weakness, such as shortness of breath, a tendency to faint, hook worms, round worms, ringing of the ears, Eye-Crosserosis, liver flukes, inflamation of the galoot, tired blood, or heartburn—DON'T READ THE REST OF THIS CHAPTER.

Just skip over it. It ain't worth the risk unless you're in top physical condition and you're mentally prepared for a tale that will make your hair stand on end.

This mission was so dangerous that I can't even reveal if I survived it or not. So there you are. Proceed at your own risk, and if you get the liver scared out of you, don't blame me.

We drove through Dead Cow Gate and headed north on a narrow, bumpy feed trail. Since we were pulling a stock trailer, Loper had to take it slow. I know that broke his heart because he loves to hot-rod the pickup over the ranch.

He's sure hard on equipment.

Well, we came to that hill that leads down to the windmill, and we inched our way down. I noticed that the Mysterious Brown Rain had stopped by this time and I went back to my position on the spare tire. Up ahead, standing near the water tank, was a horned cow, and ten-twelve feet to the west, lying in a clump of grass, was her calf.

Maybe she thought that calf was hidden, and I expect that most ordinary dogs would have missed it, but my eyes are trained to pick up the smallest details and that's just what they did.

So the clues were falling into place. We hadn't even arrived on location, yet already I had begun gathering clues and sifting evidence. I had a feeling that it wouldn't take me long to wrap this one up.

Loper stopped the pickup and he and Slim stepped out. The cow watched their every move, which was okay because I watched HER every move. She sniffed the air and bawled and looked over toward the calf. She backed up a few steps and started pawing up dirt.

So. We had one here that was going to play the tough-guy routine. I've seen it many times in my career, and I have my little bag of tricks that I use on cows like her. Sometimes I bite their heels, sometimes I bite them on the flanks, sometimes I take a killer hold on their noses, but in all cases I use quickness and superior intelligence to beat them at their own shabby game.

But here's the thing to remember: when one goes to pawing up dirt, it does something to me, inflames me, gets me all stirred up, makes me want to dive out of the pickup and go on the attack.

Which is sort of what I did. I flew out of the pickup like an arrow on its way to the target, hit the ground running, and went into what we call the Pre-Gather Barkeration Mode. Behind the complex technical language lies a simple truth, which is that a lot of times you can accomplish your primary objectives with a stern barking.

Now where were we? Oh yes, I had just dived out of the pickup and gone into the Pre-Gather Barkeration Mode. I gave her three rapid barks as a way of beginning the procedure and testing her resolve.

You might say that her resolve tested out pretty high. I knew I had a bad cow here when she answered my first three barks by loading me up on her horns and throwing me a distance of, shall we say, something in the 10-12 foot range.

In the business, we refer to this as Pre-Gather Flying Lessons. That's kind of an inside joke, see, because we rarely plan it that way, for obvious reasons. But the fact that it's an inside joke doesn't necessarily mean that it's funny.

Basically, it's not funny at all. Basically, it hurts.

You might say that she caught me slightly off guard and that landing on my back did nasty things to my ability to breathe and see. I staggered to my feet and waited for the cowboys to come my rescue.

"HANK, YOU IDIOT, LEAVE THE COW ALONE! You've got her so stirred up, we won't be able to do a thing with her!"

HUH? Leave the. . . . Well, hey, I can take a hint. By George, it doesn't take a full orchestra and a neon sign to get a point across to Hank the Cowdog. I dragged my powerful but wounded body out of the field of battle and took cover, so to speak, behind the pickup.

Loper had taken a catch rope out of the cab, and I listened as they discussed their next move. It appeared that, for reasons unknown at that point, they wanted to load the cow and calf into the trailer. How did they plan to do that out in the pasture, where they had no pens or loading facilities?

Here's what they did. Loper shook out a little loop and slipped around behind the calf. The old cow watched him and appeared ready to charge, but just then Slim stepped out and waved his hat at her. (It's an old trick, used to distract a cow on the fight.)

While the cow made wicked noises at Slim, Loper was able to get into throwing range of the calf. When the calf jumped up to run, he brought up the loop, whipped it around one time, and flipped it out. (It's called a hoolihan toss and Loper can do it pretty well.)

The loop went straight to the mark and pulled down on the calf's neck. When Calfie hit the end of the twine, he jumped into the air and started bawling. That got the old lady stirred up something terrible. Say, fellers, she was ready to do some serious damage.

She wasn't paying attention to Slim any more. She had her wild eyes on the guy who was messing around with her calf. She shook her horns and bellered and took aim for High Loper, who was trying to drag the calf to the trailer.

It was at that precise moment that Slim unleashed a secret weapon, his deadly fighting and barking machine. He looked down at me and said, "Get her, Hank!"

Even though I was still hurting from my first encounter with the nasty wench, even though I had been called an "idiot" by the very cow-boy I was being sent out to rescue, I forgave past mistakes and ignored the throbbing of my body and went streaking into combat.

I wish you could have seen it. Oh, that was an attack to remember! I sank my teeth into her brisket and suddenly she lost interest in what Loper was doing. She slung me around and bellered and slobbered, but you know what? When you got one by the brisket, she has a real hard time putting her horns to use.

Well, while old Sookie was trying to sweep the ground with me, Loper dragged the calf into the trailer, stuck it in the front compartment, and closed the middle gate. By this time I had figgered out their strategy. They'd locked the calf in the front and hoped that when the old lady heard him bawling, she would jump into the back compartment. They could close the back gate on her and that would be the end of it.

Not a bad plan, actually, only it didn't work. The old cow was so stirred up by then, she had lost interest in her calf and all she could think of was making hamburger out of me. How foolish of her, but nobody ever said that cows were smart.

Well, I played my deal about as slick as it could be played. I hung on to her brisket until

71

all hands were safe and all our objectives had been accomplished. Then I simply released my jaws and walked away.

All right, maybe I RAN away, for the simple reason that she came after me with them horns. That's an excellent reason for running. Before you could say "osmosis" five times, I had scooted my bad self under the pickup and was through for the day.

Mission accomplished.

I was ready to go to the house but the cowboys were still puzzling over the problem of how to get the cow loaded. That being their problem, I didn't concern myself with it.

I was licking down a couple of spots where the cow had mussed my coat, when all at once I realized that the boys had stopped talking. And they were looking under the pickup. At me.

"Here, Hankie, come here, boy." That was Loper. I hardly recognized his voice. Instead of yelling and cursing, he was addressing me in a tone that was not only friendly, but also full of respect and admiration.

What was this? You mean after years and years of being yelled at and taken for granted, I was suddenly getting some of the appreciation I so richly deserved?

I crawled out from under the pickup and collected kind words, pats on the head, a couple of nice rubs under my chin. I was basking, so to speak, in the limelight when . . . that was

G.L.Holmes

strange. Loper picked me up and carried me into the back compartment of the trailer, and Slim slipped the catch rope around my middle, just behind my front legs, and he pitched the coils of the rope over the bars on the left side of the . . .

What were these guys . . .

And then they left me in there by myself and Slim took hold of the rope and gave it a jerk and I went up into the air and . . .

What the heck were they . . .

"All right, Hank, start barking again, see if you can get her to come after you."

Start barking . . . see if I could . . . HUH?

Suddenly the pieces of the puzzle . . . hey, those guys were planning to use me for BAIT! Which was too bad because I had no intention of, but on the other hand, when they've got you on a catch rope, it's hard to argue . . .

I barked a protest. I mean, this was by George outrageous, but barking might not have been a smart thing to do, don't you see, because it sort of called attention to my presence there in the trailer.

And here she came. I could see the blood vanes, blood vaynes, blood vaens, spelling has never been one of my better areas, blood veins standing out on her eyeballs. I could hear her snorting like a locomotive. I could see the sharp tips of her horns gleaming in the sunlight.

Fellers, she flew into that trailer like a jungle cat and all at once it seemed awful crowded. There for a minute, I thought the old curtain was about to fall on my life's performance, so to speak, and that I was fixing to go to my internal reward.

In a flash, Loper slammed the back gate shut, which was not what I considered good news at that point, since it locked me and that wild horned woman in a small space that was getting smaller by the minute.

And at the same moment, just as I was about to be shredded and punctured, Slim jerked the rope and pulled me out of the pit of death.

"Good job, Hankie, nice work." He patted me on the head.

Many words and thoughts marched across the vast expanse of my mind at that moment, none of which I can repeat. The point is, I had survived the ordeal but it had left a bitter taste in my mouth. A bitter taste is better than no taste at all, but it's still a long way from sweet.

We loaded up and headed for the house.

Oh, one last thing. That Mysterious Brown Rain? Tobacco juice.

NO BARREL OF FUN

We got back down to the place around lunchtime. Slim and Loper unloaded the cow and calf in the heifer trap and parked the rig in front of the house. And they went inside to eat.

No more pats on the head for me. No more "thanks, Hank" or "nice job, Hank." They'd got what they needed out of me (temporary cow bait) and now they were ready to move along to something else (a nice big hot meal).

Okay, if that was the way they were going to operate, I had some things to do myself. Somebody had to look after the ranch while certain unnamed persons stuffed themselves and sat around bragging about their exploits.

Furthermore, it suddenly occurred to me

that the previous evening, I had fallen heir to a fortune and that . . . holy cats, I had to get down to the trash barrels before somebody set them on fire!

I went streaking down the hill, expecting at any moment to see the white wisp of smoke that would tell me my financial empire lay in ruins, like so much burned garbage in a barrel.

But luck was with me this time. I found the barrels just as I had left them, three of them in a row, and none was on fire. Now all I had to do was remember which one contained my Priceless Corncob: left, right, or middle?

Funny, I couldn't remember. All at once they looked pretty muchly the same. I studied the situation and decided on the middle one. Yes, that was the one. I remembered now.

A lot of dogs think you can't search a garbage barrel without turning it over. They go in with no plan, no techniques, no understanding of the physical forces involved, and what they end up with is a big mess: barrels turned over, garbage scattered over five acres, the whole nine yards.

Well, that's unnecessary. Furthermore, it's the mark of an amateur. Your trained professional cowdog will follow a set of procedures, process the garbage in a neat, efficient manner, find what he's looking for, and leave no clues behind.

I don't suppose I need to say which method I use in my work.

I took up my position, went into the deep crouch situation, thought through my jump, took my measurements, and made my calculations. Then and only then did I go into the jump procedure.

I jumped and . . .

You know, one thing a guy never thinks about when he's concentrating on higher mathematics and complex formulas is what might happen if the barrel turned out to be *empty.*

I mean, it's reasonable to assume that a garbage barrel contains garbage, right? Otherwise it would be kind of silly to be jumping into it. In security work, we seldom enter empty barrels, for the simple reason that emptiness in and of itself contains very little of interest to us.

However, what I'm sort of driving at in a round-about manner is that every once in a great while a guy jumps into a barrel that is empty. This always comes as a shock. I mean, we don't train for this type of situation because . . .

Instead of landing on a soft heap of newspapers, I plunged into the inner darkness and landed hard at the . . . well, at the bottom, of course, down there amongst the egg shells and the coffee grounds.

Obviously I had picked the wrong barrel. Obviously Slim had thrown my Priceless Corncob into one of the other two. Obviously I was trapped in a stinking trash can. And obviously I didn't intend to spend the rest of my life there.

In other words, I needed to get out. I was studying on this latest problem when a face appeared in the circle of daylight above me. It was the face of a cat: a smirking, sniveling, insolent, unbearable cat.

"My, my. You've finally found your place in this world."

"Step easy, cat, I'm in no mood for your mouth."

He lifted his right paw and gave it several long, slow strokes with his tongue. "Oh Hankie, you'll never guess what I found in this other barrel."

There was something in his tone of voice that made me just a little bit . . .

"HUH? Maybe you'd better tell me what you

found in the other barrel, and be quick about it."

He wasn't quick about it, not at all. He crouched down on the rim and started purring and twitching the end of his tail. As you know, I hate that tail-twitching business.

"I found a corncob. Isn't that a coincidence?"

A growl began deep in my throat and was amplified by the emptiness of the barrel. "No, it's not a coincidence. That's MY Priceless Corncob and you know it."

"Well, maybe it was yours, Hankie, but . . ."

"It was mine, it is mine, it always will be mine!"

He closed his eyes and purred and smiled. "Finders keepers, losers weepers. What's to keep me from taking it away and hiding it . . . from you?"

All at once, his tail dipped down into the barrel and began twitching just a few feet from the end of my nose. Up to this point, I had remained cool-headed and rational. But this latest provocation brought our relationship to an all-time low, and I could no longer take responsibility for what happened.

I leaped upward and snapped, and missed and fell back amongst the eggs shells. I leaped again and again, trying my very best to amputate his tail, but each time he managed to snatch it back.

And the whole time, he sat there looking down and grinning, just as though he had planned all along to get me stirred up, just as though I had been suckered into his shabby little game.

What he didn't know was that . . . okay, maybe I did get suckered into his shabby little game, but sometimes a guy loses his iron discipline . . .

"Give me my Priceless Corncob, you nincompoop cat!" I made another snap at his tail and, you might say, missed again.

"Come and get it, Hankie. It's right over here in this other barrel. All you have to do is jump out."

I stared up at him. He grinned down at me. He didn't think I could do it. He thought he was perfectly safe up there on his perch. Well, hey, he had made a very serious mistake in judgment because what he had seen up to that point was just my warm-up routine.

"All right, cat, you asked for it and now you're fixing to get it."

He yawned. That was a mistake too.

I went into my deepest crouch and exploded in an upward direction. I'm proud to report that I knocked Pete off his perch, sent him flying to the ground, landed in the next garbage barrel, pulled it over, hit the ground running, and chased Kitty-Kitty up the nearest tree—all in the space of just a few action-packed seconds.

I didn't bother to taunt the cat. There would be plenty of taunt for timing once I had rescued my Priceless Corncob from the garbage.

I rushed back to the barrel, which was now on the ground, and began digging through the trash: newspapers, bean cans, ketchup bottles, butcher paper, diapers . . . ah ha! There it was, my Priceless Corncob, my ticket to the future, my . . .

"HANK, GET OUT OF THE GARBAGE, YOU NASTY DOG!!"

Huh?

I wonder how Sally May . . . she seemed pretty steamed up about the . . . it did look pretty bad, I guess. I mean, the wind had come up out of the south and you might say that a lot of those newspapers had begun . . . several pages had blown into the yard and others were on their way to . . . and then the bean cans rolling around in the wind . . . yes, it looked pretty . . . it sort of detracted from the overall appearance of the . . .

I couldn't blame her for being mad. I was mad too. My only complaint was that, in a moment of anger, she misinterpreted the evidence and blamed ME for the entire mess, which probably explains why she threw the ketchup bottle at me.

Well, you know me. I can take a hint. I grabbed up my Priceless Corncob and vanished into the night. Okay, it wasn't night, it was broad daylight, but that didn't keep me from vanishing.

I had solved the Case of the Garbage Barrel, but it had been no barrel of fun.

One final note before we move on. Every once in a while, I get the feeling that Pete is involved in some kind of conspiracy. I've noticed, not once but several times, that at the very moment he has provoked me into outskirts of temper and awkward situations, Sally May shows up.

How does a dumb cat end up on the right side so often? It can't possibly have anything to do with intelligence, so how do you explain it?

Beats me. Dumb luck, I guess.

CHAPTER

9

I'M RICH!

Well, I had more important things to do than sit around and speculate about dumb cats and their uncanny ability to walk into a thorny situation and come out smelling like a rose, so to speak.

They say that if you throw a cat into the air, he'll always land on his feet. Maybe so. If I didn't have more important things to do, I wouldn't mind studying that situation in detail, especially the part about throwing cats into the air.

I'd like to spend about two weeks throwing Pete into the air, and I wouldn't care if he landed on his feet or on his nose. Your serious scientific minds don't care how their research comes out. They're in it strictly for the love of knowledge.

A little humor there.

But as I was saying, I had better things to do than . . . yes, I already said that. Shucks, I was RICH! And I mean filthy, stinking, rolling-in-the-chips kind of rich. Why, there was no calculating how much that Priceless Corncob was worth.

G.L. Holmes

When Sally May appeared on the scene and that situation at the garbage cans went sour, I picked up my little old Priceless Corncob and vanished myself down to the corrals. By this time I was feeling mighty good. In fact, I felt a song tugging at the shoestrings of my heart . . . heartstrings of my . . . I felt a song in my heart, is the point, and never mind about the strings.

Most of the time, when I feel a song in my heart, what I do about it is just by George sing it, and after setting my Priceless Corncob down along the fence in the front lot, I took a few steps back, tuned up, and burst into song. Here's how it went.

I'm Rich

Well not so very long ago, it's been just
    a day or three,
I had me a job, pretty good job, as Head
    of security.
I worked real hard, took care of my
    place, kept it safe and sound.
I knew that ranch like the back of my
    hand, I knew my way around.

I guess you could say that I was content
to leave things where they stood.
I mean, there might have been a better
deal around, but this one was pretty
good.
But then, you know, by George, one
night I fell heir to a treasure,
An Incredible Priceless Corncob, worth
more than you could measure.

And now I'm rich, you bet I'm rich!
No more sleeping in the ditch, old pal,
because I'm rich.

Well, sudden wealth can do a lot to
change your attitude.
Makes you aware of who you are and
what you have to prove.
I mean, you just can't go on living in
your same old low class style,
You've got to put on airs and flaunt
your wealth and strut your stuff a
while.

For one thing, it ain't proper now to
speak to just anyone,
You've got to choose your friends more
carefully, according to how much mun

They've got, 'cause see, a lot of dogs
   don't have it and probably never will,
And them's the kind you leave behind
   when you're marching up the hill.

'Cause now I'm rich, I'm by George
   rich.
No more sleeping in the ditch, old pal,
   this dog is rich.

Another thing you've got to watch when
   you join the upper crust
Is working eighty hours a week and
   thinking that you must.
'Cause when you've got a fortune behind you every day,
You don't even need a job to prove that
   you're okay.

There's lots of ways of acting to get
   your point across
That now you're rich and famous and
   you've become the boss.
But the best way to express your wealth
   and make it really sting
Is to stay in bed, cover up your head,
   and never do a thing!

It says you're rich! Oh, you're rich!
No more digging a ditch, pal, this dog is
    rich!

Boy, it was a crackerjack of a song! I mean, beautiful music, meaningful words, an important message, the whole nine yards.

I didn't realize I had an audience until I had finished the song, and at that point I heard a crackling in some weeds over by the loading chute and saw—not Pete the Barncat, as you might have suspected, but little Mister Half-Stepper.

He poked his head out of the weeds. "What was that all about?"

"What do you think it was all about? It was about wealth, money, riches, treasure, my fortune in Priceless Corncobs, and my new status as one of the ten wealthiest dogs in the world, speaking of which, don't get too close to my Priceless Corncob."

"Oh, okay."

"It's not that I don't trust you, Drover, it's just that you can't be trusted."

He looked at my treasure and walked around it. "Don't you think you're acting kind of silly about all this?"

"Silly? Who's acting silly? I don't know what you're talking about."

He looked up at the clouds. "I don't think corncobs are very beautiful. I don't think they're beautiful at all. I think they're ugly."

"I see. Is that all?"

"No, there's more. I don't think they're worth anything and I don't think you're rich."

"Are you finished now?"

"No, there's one more thing." All at once, he burst into tears. "Oh Hank, I went to sleep last night with my corncob right in front of my paws and when I woke up this morning, it was gone and there were coon tracks all around!"

"Wait a minute, hold it right there! Notice the clues, Drover. There's a pattern here. It's all fitting together."

"I know, I . . ."

"Shut up. It's all coming clear now: an un-guarded treasure vanishes in the night and we find coon tracks all around the scene of the crime. Don't you see what this means?"

"Yeah . . ."

"Then shut up. This means that while you slept, a band of outlaw coons slipped onto the place and stole your Priceless Corncob right from under your nose!"

"It wasn't exactly under my nose . . ."

"If you'll shut your little trap, Drover, I'll finish explaining what has happened here. You relaxed your guard, the coons made off with your treasure, and now you're a penniless bankrupt and a pauper."

The tears began to flow again. "I was afraid you'd say that! That's why I didn't want to tell you the truth. I'm never going to tell the truth again. It always gets me into trouble."

I paced up and down in front of him. "The root of your problem, Drover, is not that you told the truth, but that the truth was true. If it hadn't been so true, you wouldn't be in this mess right now."

"Yeah, but if I'd lied, it wouldn't have been true at all."

"Of course not, because a lie can't possibly be the truth. But lying bears bitter fruit. Have you heard of bitter fruit?"

"You mean chinaberries?"

"No, I don't mean chinaberries. I'm talking about the philosophical concept of bitter fruit."

He gave me a blank stare. "Are you saying that the coons ate chinaberries before they stole my corncob?"

Sometimes, when you look into Drover's eyes, you get the feeling that there is *absolute-*

ly nothing behind them, and at that point you wonder if communication is worth the effort.

"Yes, that's what I'm saying, Drover. The coons ate chinaberries and that explains why they stole your Priceless Corncob. Is it clear now?"

"It's starting to make a little sense."

"Good. Now let me finish. You were robbed and now you're broke, but instead of taking it with grace and dignity, you tried to convince me that my Priceless Corncob was worthless, in hopes I might cast it away and join you in poverty."

"How'd you know that's what I was trying to do? I thought I was being pretty sneaky."

I couldn't help chuckling. "Drover, Drover! Son, in my years of security work, I've gone up against the best crinimal minds in the business. You may not be the dumbest dog I've ever known, but you definitely rank in the Top Ten."

He wagged his tail. "Gosh, thanks, Hank. I feel better already."

"That's good, Drover, and I'm glad to have played a small part in guiding you through a difficult period of self-realization."

"Yeah, it was pretty tough there for a while."

"Of course," I examined the claws on my right foot, "you understand that I can't speak to you any more, and we can't be seen together."

"We can't?"

I shrugged. "We belong to different social classes, Drover. I'm a very wealthy dog, but you? Well, you're back to being a common ranch mutt. I'm sorry."

"Oh, that's all right, you couldn't help it."

"I have to think of my position, my status, my reputation—speaking of which, I hope you understand that I'm resigning my position with the Security Division."

"What?"

"Indeed. It wouldn't be proper for me to be engaged in common labor, would it now? And furthermore, I must see to my investments."

He stared at me and twisted his head around. "You sure are talking funny. Where'd you get that British accent?"

"It comes with wealth and high station. Furthermore, my line traces back to noble English blood."

"All that from one corncob? Mine didn't work that well on me."

"Yours, Drov-ah, had less to work *with*."

This conversation was curt shot . . . cut

short, that is, when all of a sudden we heard a strange jingling sound approaching from the east.

The cowboys had finished their lunch and were coming down to the pens.

CHAPTER

10

EARLY RETIREMENT

Quick as a snake, I pounced on my Price-less Corncob. I mean, I'd never known Slim and Loper to steal anything, but when a guy moves into the higher echelons, he must assume that everyone is a potential thief.

When they came into the corrals, I was there by the fence with my life's savings between my paws. Loper noticed, and he being the World's Leading Expert On Everything, he had to make a smart remark about it.

"Look at that fool dog. He had that corncob this morning. Do you suppose he eats those things?"

Slim stopped and stared at me. "Beats me. I think he could use a brain transplant."

They chuckled and walked down the alley to the back lot. We're so lucky to have such gifted comedians on the ranch. They're not real good at digging post holes or working cattle or working at anything, but they do have a gift for making smart-mouth remarks.

I glanced over at Drover. "What are you grinning about?"

"Who me? I don't know. Just thought it was a good time to grin, I guess."

"If I had just frittered away my fortune and lost my Priceless Corncob, I don't think I'd be grinning."

"I don't think I would either."

"Then why don't you wipe that stupid grin off your face?"

"Oh. Okay." He ran a paw over his mouth, and as though by magic, the stupid grin was replaced by a stupid frown.

Next thing I knew, a bunch of steers came pounding into the front lot. The cowboys had driven them up from the sick pen. I snatched up my Priceless Corncob and crawled through the fence. Slim backed the stock trailer up to the loading chute and he and Slim started driving the steers into the crowding pen.

They whistled and shouted, and then Slim hollered out, "Come on, Hank, give us a hand!"

Under ordinary circumstances, I'm in charge

of loading cattle, which is a sub-division of my overall position as Head of Ranch Security. Over the years I've developed a number of techniques that have revolutionized the field of cattle loading.

But that's under ordinary circumstances. On that particular day, at that particular moment, I was busy guarding my Priceless Corncob.

"Hank, come on!"

Drover was getting nervous and started hopping up and down. "Hank, they're calling. Don't you think we'd better go help?"

"You go help. I'm busy. Furthermore, I've gone into retirement."

"Retirement!"

I gave him a disgusted look. "Yeah, retirement. Maybe you've forgotten, son, I'm rich. I can do anything I want to do, and you know what I want to do?"

"What?"

"Absolutely nothing. I don't have to put up with this lousy job anymore. Maybe you have to do menial labor but I don't. From now on, I'm living on Easy Street."

"I don't even know what 'mean old labor' is, so how can I do it?"

"Just go bite a steer, that's all."

"What if he kicks me?"

"Spit out your teeth and gum him."

"Oh my gosh!" Drover hopped around in a circle, then went through the fence and crept up to the loading chute. He nipped at one of the steers, and when the brute kicked at him, he went screaming into the calf shed.

I just shook my head. I mean, I had trained the mutt. If I hadn't already gone into retire-

G.L. Holmes

ment, I would have given him a terrible tongue-lashing.

"HANK, YOU SORRY RASCAL, GET OVER HERE!!"

Sorry rascal? To who or whom were they speaking? I looked around and, seeing no sorry rascals, stayed exactly where I was, with the Priceless Corncob between my paws.

Well, without me in charge of the loading procedure, things went to pot—which, I might add, was not exactly the biggest surprise of the year. Three steers hopped into the trailer, but then they turned around and went back out. Within minutes, the entire bunch was moving in the wrong direction.

Loper picked a hedge apple off the ground and fired it at me. At ME! Well, hey, I had planned to stick around and supervise the rest of the loading process, but I wasn't going to sit there and put up with their childish tantrums.

I just by George picked up my Priceless Corncob and moved out. I was prepared to leave it at that, I mean, I had no particular objections to retiring on the ranch and giving them the benefit of my advice and presence, but they squalled nasty things at me and threw some more hedge apples.

Okay. Fine. If that's the way they wanted it,

I had other places to go. I pointed my nose to the north, trotted up the hill, past the yard gate, and went out to find the wide wonderful world.

And so it was that I turned my back on the ranch I had managed and loved for many years, never to return, a victim of sharp tongues and misunderstanding. When will people ever learn . . . oh well, what did I care?

"I'm rich, you bet I'm rich,
No more sleeping in the ditch, old pal, this
   dog is RICH!"

The song said it all. With my fortune, I didn't need the dumb ranch anymore, or the people or the crushing responsibility or any of the rest of it. I was on my way to Easy Street.

I hadn't gone more than, oh, a quarter mile when I got the feeling that I was being followed. I glanced around and, sure enough, there was Little Drover behind me, huffing and puffing to catch up.

I didn't bother to slow down. Why should I? I had important things on my mind. Nevertheless, he caught up with me.

"Hi, Hank, where you going?"

"I han't halk wuff iss horn hob ing eye owff."

"Oh. Well, I was headed that way myself. I guess we might as well go together."

"I han't halk wuff iss horn hob ing eye owff, you unce!"

"Thanks. You look pretty good yourself."

I stopped and placed my Priceless Corncob

G.L. Holmes

on the ground. "I said, I can't talk with this corncob in my mouth, you dunce."

He stared at me and twisted his head. "What corncob? I thought you just took it out of your mouth."

"I did just take it out."

"Oh. Then why can't you talk to me?"

"I am talking to you!"

"Oh. I thought you were, but then you said . . ."

"Never mind what I said! Where do you think you're going?"

"Who me? I don't know, just tagging along. Where do you think you're going?"

"I'm going to a resort community where I can sit in the sun and enjoy my wealth."

"What a coincidence! That's where I'm going too."

"Oh no you're not. In the first place, I travel light and alone. In the second place, I don't want to be responsible for a mental invalid."

"So far, we agree on everything."

"In the third place, I shouldn't even be talking to you. I have my social position to think about now."

"Okay, you think about that and I'll think about the clouds, and then we'll all have something to think about and that'll make the trip seem shorter."

I could only shake my head in wondermentation. "You missed the whole point, Drover, but that's nothing new."

"No, but that doesn't make it any less old."

"I can't take you with me, do you understand that? Someone might think we were friends."

"Don't worry about it, Hank. That's what friends are for."

"No! You can't go, period!" His head began to sink and he got that pitiful look in his eyes. I guess I'm a sucker for pitiful looks. "Unless . . ." His head came up. "Unless you would consider going along as my valet."

All at once he was jumping up and down. "Oh sure, Hank, that would be just fine! I don't know much about dancing but I can sure learn."

"All right. The main thing is, you have to follow orders and address me as 'Your Lordship.' "

"Sure. I can do that, Hank."

"Your Lordship."

"Oh, you can just call me Drover, I don't mind, just plain old Drover."

"That's what I said, you cretin."

"Oh. I thought you called me Your Lordship."

"No, that's what you call ME."

"I thought I called you Hank."

"You did, you nincompoop, but you're supposed to address me as Your Lordship."

"My Lordship?"

"No, YOUR Lordship!"

"That's what I said. I thought that's what I said. What did I say?"

"When?"

"Right before you said what you said."

"What did I say?"

"You called me a cretin. What's a cretin?"

"Who cares what a cretin is?"

"Not me, I can tell you that."

"Then quit asking stupid questions! You're my valet and . . . by the way, what was that stuff you said about dancing?"

"Me? I didn't say anything about dancing."

"You did say something about dancing. Don't deny it."

"Okay, I won't deny it."

I waited. "Well? Why did you bring up dancing?"

"Who me? I didn't . . . oh yeah, maybe I

did, I sure did, but I don't think I ought to tell you."

"Tell me, and be quick about it."

"Oh rats. Okay. Well Hank . . ."

"Your Lordship."

"Just call me Drover."

"GET TO THE POINT ABOUT DANCING!"

"Well . . . I want to be your valet but I don't know much about dancing."

I studied the runt for a long time, searching for signs of intelligent life. I didn't find any. "All right, Drover, I give up. Tell me what being a valet has to do with dancing."

"I don't know. I've just heard about valet dancing . . ."

"Drover," I moved closer and looked deeply into his eyes, "is this a pathetic attempt to be funny? Are you trying to make jokes or are you merely wasting my valuable time?"

"Which would you rather?"

Suddenly I felt exhausted, as though I had been walking for ten days through quicksand. "Never mind. Pick up my Priceless Corncob and let's get out of here."

He did, and we moved out, heading north toward the caprock. "Now, one last time, Drover, do you understand your job?"

"I han't halk wuff wis horn hob ing eye outh."

"No thanks, not until we reach our destination, but I appreciate your asking."

"I han't halk wuff wis horn hob ing eye outh, you unce."

"Very good. At last we understand one another. Communication, Drover, that's what this life is all about."

It was a beautiful afternoon for a walk across the prairie. But little did we know what dangers lay ahead. If we had, then we would have known.

C H A P T E R

11

CAPTURED BY CANNIBALS

You don't expect to run into coyotes during the daylight hours. They, being lazy and shiftless brutes, usually sleep all day and venture out at night to find their bloody adventures.

Chances are, we wouldn't have run into the coyotes at all that afternoon, for just as I suspected, they were lying around in holes and behind rocks, sheeping and being sliftless . . . sleeping and being shiftless, that is, we wouldn't have run into them at all but for one small accident of coincidence.

In making our way up the caprock, we blundered right into the middle of the coyote village.

There are many places a ranch dog should

avoid. Near the top of the list is the coyote village. Not only are these wild brutes unfriendly to civilized beings, they will EAT THEM if given the slightest opportunity. We gave them more than a slight opportunity.

I knew we were in trouble when I stepped on the face of a sleeping cannibal and caused him to squall in pain. All at once I found myself looking into the flaming yellow eyes of Snort. I noticed that he had a particularly nasty expression on his face.

"Well, blow me down!" I said, never dreaming that Snort would give a literal interpretation to what I intended as friendly conversation. But he did. He struck me a blow between the eyes and I went down.

There was a lesson in this. When in the company of savages, never say, "Blow me down." Say something less inflammatory, such as, "Good afternoon" or "Fancy meeting you here." Just thought I'd toss that in.

By the time the stars cleared from my head, Snort had sounded the alarm. The village sprang to life as though by magic. Coyotes came from all directions, pouring out of holes in the ground and leaping out from behind rocks, until suddenly, Little Drover and I were not only surrounded by Snort, which would have been serious enough, but also by his uncles, aunts, cousins, brothers, sisters, nieces, nephews, and business associates.

"Hey Snort, you didn't need to wake up the whole village. We were just passing by and thought we'd stop in for . . ."

G. L. Holmes

"Stupid dog to step on Snort face. Snort not like face stepping on to be."

"Right. It was clumsy of me and I have no excuses at all and I'll have to give you a complete apology and then we'll be on our way."

Snort shook his head.

"Oh, maybe we could stay for a while. Do we have time, Drover?"

I glanced at Drover. His eyes were crossed and he was shaking like a leaf in a high wind. This was his first exposure to cannibals at close range, and he was not holding up well.

I turned back to Snort. "Sure, we've got a few minutes, what the heck, but then we really do have to . . ."

At that moment, an old, scruffy, moth-eaten coyote pushed his way through the crowd, and when he saw me, his eyes lit up. "Ah ha! Ranch dog come at berry good time."

This was old Many-Rabbit-Gut-Eat-In-Full-Moon, chief of the village, also the father of the beautiful coyote princess, Girl-Who-Drink-Blood, and her not-so-beautiful brother, Scraunch the Terrible. Old Chief Gut and I had done business before, and he wasn't a half-bad fellow—for a cannibal, you understand.

"Well, thank you, Chief Gut. I was afraid

we'd interrupted your naps and we could sure come back another time if . . ."

"Oh no! Time good, yes?" He glanced around the crowd. The other coyotes nodded their heads and licked their chops, which I took to be not such a good sign. "Oh yes, time berry good. Billage not have plans for supper before you coming. Now billage have BIG plan for supper, oh boy!"

The crowd yipped and howled. "Well, as I was telling my good friend Snort, we just dropped in to say howdy and see how the kids are doing and . . ."

"Kids hungry."

"Yes, I bet they are, growing and everything, but we . . ."

"Need big grub."

"Boy, they do eat, don't they, but anyway, as I was saying, Drover, start backing out of here, and whatever you do, don't drop my Priceless Corncob."

There is a certain predictability in Drover's behavior. No doubt if I had told him to spit out the Priceless Corncob at once, he would have held it to the death. Since I told him to hang on to it, he let if fall from his lips, and then he fainted. The little dunce.

Quick as a flash, I snatched the treasure out of the dust. I would have preferred being subtle about it, don't you see, but it didn't work out that way. I had to grab it, and drat the luck, Old Man Gut noticed.

His eyes widened. "What that?"

"Oh, uthing, ust an ol horn hob."

"What saying? Not understand." I said it again. "Not talk with mouth full!"

"Oh." I set the treasure down between my paws. "I said it's nothing, just a smelly old corncob, nothing you'd be interested in. In other words, nothing. Really. Honest. I'm serious."

Chief Gut extended his neck toward my treasure and sniffed the air. "Not believe it nothing. Must be something."

I tried to cover it up with my paws. "Oh, not really, Chief. Say, where's that pretty daughter of yours?"

"Out hunting. What you cover up with paws?"

"Paws? What paws? Oh, these? Heck, they're the same old paws I had last time I was here."

Just then, two things happened. Drover woke up, and a big, nasty-looking gray coyote warrior pushed his way through the crowd.

He looked a lot like . . . Scraunch. In fact, he WAS Scraunch. Uh oh.

Drover sat up. "Where am I? Which way's the machine shed? Oh, my leg hurts!"

Scraunch wasted no time with small talk. He lumbered over to Drover and showed him some fangs. All at once Drover's eyes looked like plates with little black dots in the center.

"Little White Dog answer Scraunch question pretty quick."

"Oh my gosh!"

"Drover," I said, "don't tell them anything. Just keep your little trap shut about the T-R-E-A-S-U-R-E."

Scraunch growled and Drover began to shake. "Little White Dog talk!"

"Oh my gosh, all right, I'll talk, what do you . . ."

"Drover! Don't say a word about the Priceless Corncob!" Every eye turned to me. You might say that I had let the cat out of the sand box. I turned to Old Man Gut and tried to smile. "You probably thought I said 'Priceless Corncob,' but that's not what I said at all. At the very least, that's not what I *meant* to say . . . don't you see."

My explanation wasn't selling. I could see it in their eyes. A nasty little smile twitched across Scraunch's mouth and he went nose-to-nose with Little Mister Saucer Eyes.

"What means, Priceless Corncob? Better you talking fast."

"Talking fast . . . oh my gosh, Hank, I think I'm fixing to . . . it's a Priceless Corncob, it's worth a fortune, Hank's the richest dog in the world!"

Scraunch smiled and walked over to me. "What means 'fortune?' "

"Fortune? Oh, it doesn't mean, you can't believe anything Drover . . ." He raised his lips and showed me those long, sharp teeth. Pretty impressive at close range. "What I mean is, I'm one of the richest dogs in the entire world. I mean, I have wealth, power, influence, you name it. And I guess you know what that means."

Scraunch and Chief Gut shook their heads. "Well, it would be very dangerous for you to mess around with anyone who owned a Priceless Corncob. Don't you see."

Now their heads nodded and I noticed a certain gleam in their yellow eyes. Then Scraunch tapped himself on the chest. "Scraunch own Priceless Corncob now."

"Ah ha, to wait one small minute!" said Chief Gut, tapping himself on the chest.

"Priceless Fortunate Cob belong to *Chief,* not to son of Chief."

Then Snort stepped forward. "Uh! Snort think Snort deserve Cornless Fortunate Cob because Snort catch dog in village!"

Then another big ugly coyote stepped forward. "Too much being greedy. Cobless Corn Fortune belong whole village, divide up for every coyote rich and famous to become!"

Well, that did it. You ever see a bunch of cannibals fighting over money? Within seconds, them coyotes had started one of the biggest riots in Ochiltree County history, and we're talking about men, women, and children, fellers, the whole by George village. The air was so full of dust and coyote hair that you could hardly see . . .

You could hardly see anything, so why was I just standing there? "Drover, this is it, son, run for your life!"

I grabbed up the Priceless Corncob and dived off a ledge. While I was in mid-air, I turned to see if Drover was behind me. He was, but not in the way I had expected. He was so scared, he ran around in a circle and . . . I couldn't believe it. The little runt FAINTED!

I hit the ground, lost my footing, and rolled all the way to the bottom of the caprock. I got up and shook myself. Up above, I could hear the riot. I considered going back for Drover, but not for very long. It would have been a hopeless, suicidal gesture. The little mutt had had his chance and he'd muffed it.

I hated to leave my assistant in the company of hungry, unfriendly cannibals, but at least I had saved the Priceless Corncob. I mean, it sounds tacky to put it that way, but when you've got wealth, you can always buy new friends.

And so, with a heavy heart but not as heavy as it would have been if I had lost my fortune, I loped around the base of the caprock and headed north into Blind Canyon. If the coyotes came after me, they would assume I had gone south, back to headquarters. In choosing a northerly course, well, I guess you get the picture.

It was getting late in the day when I reached the seep springs near the head of the canyon, and I figured it would be safe for me to stop and rest. I laid the Priceless Corncob down in the grass and walked to the edge of the pool.

The water was clear and still, and I could see my reflection. Not a bad looking guy, in fact, just pretty by George handsome. There was something about the nose that spoke of wealth

G.L.Holmes

and power. Or was it the angle of the head? Or a certain sparkle in the eyes?

Hard to say, but the bottom line was RICH and HANDSOME, and that ain't a bad combination in this old world. I mean, give me a choice between "good and homely" and "rich and handsome" and I'll take . . .

HUH?

All at once there were two faces in the water, and I was pretty sure that only one of them belonged to me. And . . .

Uh oh. The second face looked very much like a . . . COYOTE!

12

A WILD BUT SHORT ROMANCE. ALSO AN EXCITING CONCLUSION

Well, you know me. When it comes to putting two and two together, I'm pretty rapid. If there was a coyote face reflecting in the water, then surely there was a coyote not far away.

I whirled, wondering which it would be: Scraunch, Rip, Snort, Chief Gut. I fared my bangs, bared my fangs, that is, and prepared to go into deadly combat.

Imagine my surprise when I saw . . . MERCY! Very seldom in my career had I seen a lovelier face, a prettier nose, or a more gorgeous pair of yellow-green eyes. My goodness. I was looking into the eyes of a coyote princess!

"Missy? Missy Coyote? Could it be you?"

She smiled and blinked her eyes and, holy smoke, my heart and legs just about went out on me. "What Hunk doing in deep canyon?"

"Well-uh, all of a sudden I don't remember what I was doing up here and all of a sudden I don't care. I don't know my own name or who I was before I saw your face because I was nobody before this moment."

She smiled "Hunk talk crazy."

"Oh, you talk about crazy! You ain't seen anything yet. Watch this." I leaped into the air, did a back flip, and landed on my feet. "What do you think of that? And watch this." I walked on my back legs, then jumped into the air, landed on my front legs, and walked around on them for a while. "Ever see anything quite like that?"

"Hunk act crazy as coyote."

"You better believe it, but you haven't heard me sing yet. Wait until you hear me sing, Missy, it'll knock your socks off."

"What means 'socks'?"

"It means . . . well, it means that with one single song, and I'm talking about one of my rapturous magnificent love songs, you'll know once and for all that I'm just by George wild about you."

"That mean wild like coyote?"

"Wild like wild plums and wild grass and wild hairs and a wild wind blowing through the wild canyon of my heart."

"That sound," she widened her eyes, boy, that was cute, "that sound pretty wild!"

"Sit down, Missy, grab hold of something. I feel that song working its way up to the surface." She sat down, and I sang her my song.

My Heart Goes Wild For You

My heart grows wild for you,
You're the soft caress of morning
  dew.
My heart just grows wild for you,
The fragrant earth sustains it,
The sky just can't contain it,
My heart grows wild for you.

My heart glows wild for you,
You're the sun that gives it light and
  hue.
My heart just glows wild for you.
Love's flame knows no season,
It burns both rhyme and reason,
My heart glows wild for you.

My heart goes wild for you,
Madness, rushing wind, what can I
   do?
My heart just goes wild for you,
I don't have words to name it,
I lack the will to tame it,
My heart goes wild for you.

Once I got into the song, Missy came in on some of the parts and we did a nice little duet. My goodness, she had a pretty voice, especially when you consider who her kinfolks were.

Well, we nuzzled and talked and watched the sun slip below the caprock. I had pretty muchly forgotten everything else in the world. I mean, what else was there in the world? When a guy finds the Missy Coyote of his dreams, he stops dreaming and starts living.

To tell you the truth, I'd even forgotten that I was rich and famous. Somehow that didn't matter any more. But most of all, I had forgotten Little Drover.

It was just about sundown when we heard the rustle of wings and looked up to see a buzzard sitting in a small hackberry tree not far away. It was Junior the Buzzard, and Wallace, his old man, was gliding around in circles high above us.

"Junior!" the old man yelled. "Are they dead, son? Is this the supper we've been waiting for?"

Junior squinted his eyes at us. "Uh excuse m-me, b-b-but are y-yall d-d-dead?"

I stood up, gave myself a shake, and walked over to the tree. "Sorry, Junior, but as you've already guessed, this particular supper has been cancelled. In other words, no, we ain't dead."

"Oh d-d-darn." He called up to the old man. "It's m-my d-d-doggie f-friend and h-h-h-he ain't d-d-dead."

"Then you git yourself back up here," Wallace yelled back, "it's almost dark, you've wasted enough our, it's time we went to roost and we still don't have no dinner, I never should have listened to a danged kid!"

Junior looked at me and grinned. "H-h-he's m-m-mad again." Then the grin disappeared from his . . . well, from his face, of course. "D-d-did you know th-th-that the c-c-coyotes are f-f- fixing to uh uh eat your l-little white f-f-friend?"

HUH? Holy smokes, I had completely forgotten about Little Drover! I mean, a woman like Missy Coyote can sure take your mind off your work, but still . . .

"Are you sure they're going to eat him?"

Junior nodded. "I f-f-flew over th-their v-v-village and th-th-they're having a b-b-b-big d-d-dance r-right now."

Missy had been listening and wanted to know what we were talking about. I told her the whole story. Her face became very serious and she shook her head.

"Sound berry bad for little friend."

"Yeah, that's lousy luck, all right. In many ways he wasn't such a bad little mutt. I just wish . . . "

"Must help little dog. Must help friend."

"It's no use, Missy. If I went back up there, they'd tear me to ribbons."

"Maybe Missy Coyote help. Go to village, talk to brother."

"It wouldn't work, Missy. You know how they are. You should have seen the way they were fighting over my . . . "

An idea popped into my head. I dashed over to the spring pool and looked down at my Priceless Corncob. There it lay: wealth, fame, comfort, influence, everything a dog dreams of acquiring in a lifetime. And over against that—a sawed-off, stub-tailed, pea-brained, short-haired, incompetent little mutt named Drover.

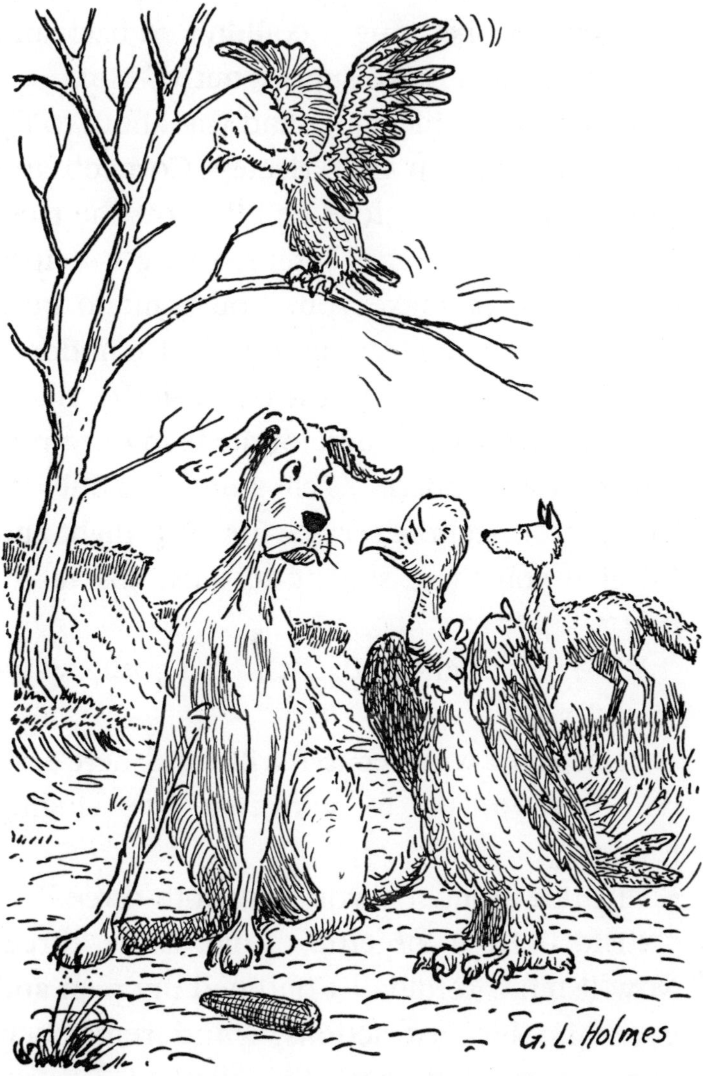
G. L. Holmes

How much was Drover worth on the open market? Very, very little. Unfortunately, he was my friend, and regardless of the dollars and cents of the thing, I couldn't sit back and let the coyotes make supper out of him.

Junior spread his wings and was about to fly off. I snatched up the Priceless Corncob and stopped him just before he lifted off the tree.

"Hold up a minute, Junior, I've got a little proposition to make you. You want to be a singer when you grow up, right?" He nodded. "And I'm a pretty impressive musician, right? And we've sung a couple of duets in our time, right?" He nodded. "Tell you what I'll do. You perform a little service for me tonight and I'll give you three singing lessons, absolutely free."

His face brightened. "Oh g-g-gosh, w-w-would you?"

"Not only will I, but I will. And here's all you have to do to win two free singing lessons."

"I th-th-thought y-you said th-th-three."

"Did I? How forgetful of me. Okay, three. Now listen carefully." I outlined my plan and gave him his instructions. "And remember, don't do anything until I've climbed the caprock and you see me in position. You got all that?"

"Wu-wu-wu-well . . . "

"Just say yes, Junior. We don't have a minute to spare."

"Y-y-y-y-y-y-y-y-y . . . okay."

Junior flapped his big wings, almost crashed into the side of a hill, but pulled out of it just in time. Then I turned to Missy and looked into her eyes.

"Well, Missy, it appears that you and I will have to wait for another time and another place. You stay here."

"But Hunk need . . ."

"No, Missy. We're different, you and I. I have my job and you have your family. We'll meet again, and until we do, you'll always be in my heart. It goes wild for you, remember?"

She nodded and gave me a sad smile. "Missy remember. Good-bye, Hunk."

"So long, Missy."

Before I could change my mind, I turned and ran down the canyon, leaping rocks, dodging trees, and listening to the crazy beat of my heart. I tried to put her out of my mind, but that wasn't easy.

The sun was down by this time and the

whole valley was slipping away in deep purple shadows. I stopped at the base of the caprock to catch my breath. Up above me, I could hear the coyote village in wild celebration. I searched the sky for Junior but didn't see him.

If he failed to do his part . . . never mind.

I started up the caprock, darting from bush to bush and rock to rock. Within minutes, I had reached the ledge I had dived off of a few hours earlier. I peeked over the ledge and there they were, ten, twenty, maybe thirty wild savage coyotes dancing in the moonlight. And in the center of it all sat Little Drover.

I glanced up at the sky and searched in vain for my buzzard friend. He wasn't there. Our plan was doomed. But then . . . suddenly TWO buzzards appeared, streaking down toward the coyote village.

"Junior, you come back here, I don't care what you, we have to go to our roost, now you quit this acting foolish or I'll . . ."

Junior was in the lead, followed by his old man. Junior followed my flight plan and made a perfect run. Diving down out of the dark sky, he began to squawk and make your typical buzzard noises. The coyotes stopped their dancing and looked up.

Perfect! Junior had their attention. At the

bottom of his arc, he released the Priceless Corncob and dropped it right in the middle of the cannibals. He wagged his wings in a gesture of farewell and flew away.

Every coyote head followed the path of the missile as it fell to the earth, and when it hit, three of the biggest and ugliest coyotes pounced on it, and fellers, the riot started all over again. Within seconds, the entire village was in an uproar.

And what did Drover do? He sat there watching the riot! I leaped up on the ledge. "Drover, come on, son, run for your life?"

He came padding over to me. "Oh, hi Hank, what are you doing?"

I didn't take time to answer. I pushed him over the ledge and jumped off behind him. We half-ran and half-rolled all the way to the bottom, jumped up, and went streaking straight south toward headquarters. We didn't slow down until we reached the mailbox north of the house.

We sat down and caught our breath. Then Drover said, "How come you were in such a big rush?"

I glared at him. "I just sacrificed my Priceless Corncob to save your worthless skin, is what all the big rush was about."

"You did?"

"Yes sir, I did. I guess you know those coyotes were fixing to eat you for supper."

"No fooling? I wondered what they were doing. They sure are rowdy, aren't they? Awful noisy."

I told him about my brilliant plan that had saved him from the coyotes. "So, as you can see, Drover, I used their own natural greed against them. It cost me a fortune, but I beat them at their own shabby game."

"Well I'll be derned. I guess we're both broke now, and I've probably lost my valet job."

"So it seems, Drover, so it seems." I looked up at the big harvest moon and sighed. The moon reminded me of Missy's eyes. "We're back to the same old job on the same old ranch."

"Yeah, but it's still the same old place."

"But maybe it's all for the best. You saw what sudden wealth did to those coyotes. It brought out all their nastiness and greed. Who knows? If I had kept that fortune, maybe it would have brought out a couple of bad qualities in me."

Drover gave me a funny look. "Oh, surely not, Hank, not you."

We trotted down to headquarters. "I know it's hard to believe, but you never can tell."

(There's more on the next page. Pretty good stuff too.)

Epiglotis

We had just passed the east side of the machine shed when I heard a familiar noise: the scraping sound a fork makes when it is pulled across a dinner plate. I called a halt and we crouched down in the weeds and looked toward the sound.

Sure 'nuff, there was Sally May leaning over the yard fence and scraping supper morsels into Pete's dish. We waited in silence. Sally May said a few words to Kitty-Kitty and went back into the house.

When the coast was clear, I pushed myself up, went into my stalking position, and crept down the hill. Speaking of greed and gluttony, Pete was so busy making a hog of himself that he never got the news until I whacked him across the backside and sent him flying into the fence. He hissed and yowled and sprinted for the nearest tree.

Drover and I fell on the scraps and devoured them. Then Drover pointed to something on the ground. "Hank, look! It's a . . . it's a Price-less Corncob!"

I went over to it and sniffed it out. It was indeed a corncob. "Yes, Drover, but we've already learned our lesson."

"Which lesson?"

"The lesson of the corncob. It was a curse, Drover. It brought trouble and misery to everyone who touched it. No, we won't even be tempted this time, will we?"

"I guess not."

"Come on, we've got a night patrol to make." I started down to the saddle shed but stopped when I realized Drover wasn't behind me. I looked back. There, in the blue glow of the mercury vapor yard light, Drover was staring down at the corncob, a wild and crazy expression in his eyes.

"Oh my gosh, I'M RICH!!"

"Whoa, hold it right there, stop, halt!" I went back and pushed him aside. "I can't allow you to do this to yourself."

"I saw it first!"

"Yes, but I saw it second, and furthermore, you're just lucky there's someone on this ranch who cares enough about you to take it off your hands and . . . "

You ever get the feeling that some stories go

135

on and on and on, repeat themselves, come up over again, and never end? I get that feeling sometimes.

So how do you end an unending story? You run out of paper, which is what I just did.

G. L. Holmes

CALLING ALL KIDS!

HERE'S YOUR CHANCE TO JOIN THE HANK THE COWDOG SECURITY SQUAD

Members of the Hank the Cowdog Security Squad receive a newsletter from Hank the Cowdog jam-packed with information about all of his latest adventures, a Hank the Cowdog warning poster, and Hank the Cowdog stickers!

Be a part of the fun! Join today! Fill out the membership information form below and send in $2 to cover the cost of postage and handling. We'll send you a Hank the Cowdog Security Squad membership package pronto!

HANK THE COWDOG SECURITY SQUAD MEMBERSHIP FORM
Please send $2 to cover postage and handling

NAME _____

ADDRESS _____

CITY _____ STATE _____ ZIP CODE _____

BOY _____ GIRL _____ WHAT GRADE ARE YOU IN? _____

WHAT SCHOOL DO YOU ATTEND? _____

HOW MANY HANK THE COWDOG BOOKS HAVE
YOU READ? _____

Please note: All Canadian and foreign orders must be payable in U.S. currency or by international money order. Please allow 2 to 4 weeks for delivery.

MAIL TO: HANK THE COWDOG SECURITY SQUAD
MEMBERSHIP
P.O. BOX 1569
AUSTIN, TEXAS 78767